HEARTLINE

FAIRHAVEN WITCHES
BOOK ONE

E. M. LEANDER

ISBN:

Hardback: 979-8-9904666-7-8

Paperback: 979-8-9949232-0-7

Ebook: B0G4NPVB87

ALSO BY E. M. LEANDER

GAME OF GODS

Wren and the Tarnished Tiger

Aris and the Obsidian Door

The Immortal Scales

and

Heirs of Flame and Frost

SPACE CAMP

The View from Ganymede

Daughters of Jupiter

Ganymede Awakens

CHAPTER 1

You should never turn your back on a sentient mistletoe.

One minute, I'm not enjoying the annual Yule party, like I do every year. The next, Marvin is following me around on the ceiling like a giant, spiky exclamation point. *Look at her, everyone! She's single! She needs to be kissed!* he seems to say.

Again.

"One of these years, I'm going to turn you into kindling," I mutter, eyeing Marvin's branches.

If the mistletoe could roll his eyes at me, he would. If he had eyes. I actually don't know how he sees or hears anything. Still, I can feel my insides shriveling at his attention, and I don't hesitate to push back.

"Honestly. You're creepy."

In response, Marvin puffs up all his leaves, making himself even larger and more impossible to miss, as if to say, *Oh, I* will *get you a kiss!*

"Oh, don't let that mean old witch scare you," Stella says, coming up and throwing an arm around my shoulders to give me a squeeze. "I won't let her touch you."

"I'm not *that* old," I mutter, squeezing my best friend back—who is in fact several years older than I am. In fact, I've only recently celebrated my twenty-ninth birthday—for the third time. I just don't appreciate being mocked by a shrub for being single. When my choices are only the dismal options left here in Fairhaven, being single is the infinitely better option.

"Marvin just likes to play matchmaker. Don't you, Marv?" Stella coos up at the mistletoe, who is hanging over our heads like a leafy disco ball.

He shakes himself back and forth adamantly, clusters of little white berries shaking like maracas. Oddly, he doesn't have roots. Mistletoe is a semiparasitic plant, I've learned from Stella. It absorbs nutrients from a host tree or shrub, while also carrying out its own photosynthesis.

Marvin feeds off my misery instead. And probably magic.

"See? He just wants you to be happy," Stella says with a dazzling smile, tucking a strand of raven hair behind her ear and sipping from her wineglass.

"You're not the one he's stalking," I groan, crossing my arms.

Stella giggles, like she always does after half a sip of alcohol, and tugs me across the room. She favors minimalist clothing, which my maximalist thread witch self has always struggled against. At least she lets me dress her daughter sometimes. Tonight Stella wears a sleek white dress, with moonstones decorating her wrists and ears. She looks like a winter queen from a fairy tale, and I'd tell her that if she wasn't being so supportive of my leafy nemesis.

Marvin follows overhead, though I stick my tongue out at him when Stella is not looking. Stella pulls me into the curve of the grand staircase, away from the crowd a little. We get some stares—or rather, I do, though no one says anything outright. Instead, they hurriedly turn their backs and whisper to each other.

"Are you sure you want to do this?" Stella says, looking over my party dress. We all dress up for Yule, wearing our finest jewels and silk and velvet and lace—and still my outfit stands out.

"Yes," I say firmly. "It's only the smallest bit of magic. Barely enough to be noticed. And look, the world hasn't ended!" I give Stella what I hope is a confident smile.

The space between her eyebrows furrows.

It really is a *tiny* amount of magic. I didn't think half the people here would even notice, though clearly I was wrong. A thrill runs through me, straightening my spine. Magic *is* still present in Fairhaven, whether the coven wants to acknowledge it or not. And if I have to bash them over the head with it to prove it—figuratively speaking—I will. And Stella knows that.

She sighs and drags me deeper into her house.

"Come on. Let's get you a drink first. You shouldn't have to face this sober."

She's really outdone herself for the Yule party this year. Her huge home is covered with delicate sparkling glass snowflakes and draping garlands of silver tinsel that throw rainbows of light on everything. As she's a healing witch, there are plants in tasteful pots all over the home too—sage, rosemary, lavender, lemongrass. Most of these carry tinsel decorations. She has large quartz obelisks displayed like pieces in a museum. An amethyst geode turned side table sits in the entry hall; an abstract obsidian sculpture decorates a bookshelf. To anyone else, these look like art.

To Stella, they resonate with her healing magic and amplify it.

Or they would, if Hartwood let her use it. I frown at the thought and turn to take in the rest of Stella's decorations.

She has a Christmas tree in the lobby, replete with silver and white decorations—to the point it can barely stand upright. An heirloom menorah perches on the mantel. A yule log of epic proportions sits in the fireplace, crackling away. And in the kitchen, a cookie jar shaped like Rudolph the Red-Nosed Reindeer plays "Jingle Bells" when opened—which Stella's teenage daughter, Ruby, does about every thirty seconds, laughing as her father chases her away from it.

It would be a lie to say that witches aren't inclusive. We celebrate *everything*, though Yule is the favorite in our town. Every year, Stella—and her decor—is voted to throw the coven's annual celebration. It may also have something to do with the fact that her husband is a fantastic chef and goes all out for the food. Even though her husband, Jacque, is human, he knows and loves Stella for what she is, and celebrates the season right along beside her. Their daughter, Ruby, has already shown some magical inclination—she once set fire to Stella's hair when she threw a tantrum as a toddler—though, of course, we won't really know until she's ready to claim her familiar, so we've got just under a year. Which reminds me.

"Where's Flossy?" I ask, changing the subject and taking a cranberry-and-champagne cocktail from Jacque with a grateful smile. He's frosted the rim with sugar crystals that look like snow. It's sweet and bubbly and will probably go immediately to my head.

"Oh, that's delicious," I sigh, earning a proud smile from Jacque.

Stella gives me a sideways look that tells me she knows I'm changing the subject, and that she doesn't agree with what I'm doing but loves me anyway. We've been best friends for our entire lives—a single look can say a lot.

"Oh, Flossy's upstairs. Ruby's been pulling her tail feathers all day, so she's hiding for now," Stella says after a moment, with a dramatic sigh.

I'm "Auntie Ivy" to Ruby, and in my eyes, she will never do wrong, not even when she's tormenting her mom's familiar. I try to hide my smile by taking another sip of my drink, though from the look on Stella's face, I'm failing miserably.

More guests arrive, the senior members of our coven, who smell like mothballs and look more like zombies than witches, and Stella leaves me to make her obligatory social rounds. I tuck a stray green curl behind my ear and think about going to help Jacque in the kitchen. It's easier than trying to socialize with people who don't particularly like me. I sip my drink and slide a little cheese cube into my pocket for Cinder, who accepts it with a grateful squeak.

When Stella was claimed by her familiar, the coven celebrated for days. Flossy—Stella knew she wanted to be a dentist since she was five years old, so the name isn't that surprising—is a scarlet macaw, which honestly has no business being in our little New England town. But now? I can't imagine the place without her. Her arrival caused a commotion among the coven for a while—witches are supposed to have cats, not macaws. A fox, maybe, or a raven. But definitely *not* a blue-and-red-and-yellow parrot.

In retrospect, that was probably when magic started misbehaving in Fairhaven.

Now Flossy talks nonsense with Stella's littlest patients at her work and flies to Marigold's bakery, Honey & Hearth, for lunch, because Marigold saves her all the unsold fruitcake this time of year. She's like an emotional support parrot for anxious dental patients, and is quite the town icon these days.

Cinder stirs in my pocket, looking for more cheese. I nab another cube from the cheese plate, and when I slip it into my pocket, I feel the tiniest nibble of teeth against my fingertip.

I'm bored, she's saying. *Let's go home.*

I want to let her out of my pocket, but even people who *know* that my familiar is a mouse—like, say, everyone in this house—tend to jump and scream or at the very least get uncomfortable when a rodent runs around. Witches are supposed to have *cats*, not mice. Plus, she's small and likely to be stepped on. Her preferred mode of transportation is riding on my shoulder, or curled up in the hood of my sweatshirt, but I've forgone the sweats tonight in favor of a dark green dress I made especially to celebrate the season. I embroidered little silver stars all over it and infused it with just enough magic to make it twinkle like the night sky. A tiny bit of insignificant magic. So very, *very* small. So why is my heart pounding like I've just run ten miles? Not that I've ever done that, but still.

Cinder nips at my finger again, and I withdraw my hand from my pocket. Madam Hartwood's black cat, Salem—I mean, *Salem?* Can we get any less original?—narrows his yellow eyes on me. He knows I have a mouse hidden somewhere. Cinder lost a tuft of fur on her back during their last encounter. The fur grew back in a lighter gray, and I catch Cinder looking at the patch from time to time, possibly plotting her revenge on the offending feline. I'm not sure exactly what the rules are about one witch's familiar eating another's, but since Madam Hartwood *is* the head of our coven, I figure the odds are never going to be in my favor.

At that moment, a mistletoe berry plinks off my head and bounces right into my drink. I look up at Marvin, who rustles innocently.

"Come *on*, Marvin. There aren't even any single warlocks here tonight!" I protest, fishing the berry out of my drink and flicking it into the sink.

Our coven, like most, is predominantly female. I've dated a few human males but never felt any real connection with them. Marvin thinks I'm being too picky. I call it having standards.

"Ah, Ivy, lovely to see you, dear. It's been too long," Madam Hartwood purrs, stroking Salem's sleek fur. From the safety of her arms, he hisses at me.

I take a large gulp of my drink.

Madam Hartwood is tall and thin, with a mole on her chin and bushy eyebrows. She and the crones following her around like puppies are all dressed in traditional witchy black, though diamonds and blood-red rubies drip from ears and fingers like bleeding icicles, and their gowns are silk and layered tulle and crushed velvet. Only Madam Hartwood stands out, austere in what is probably an original puritanical outfit from the 1690s witch trials. Not a single piece of jewelry or lace for Madam Hartwood, not even for Yule.

"Thank you, Madam Hartwood," I mumble, feeling heat rush to my cheeks. Having the attention of our coven's mother focused on me makes my insides squirm. Her gaze misses nothing.

The heat fades to ice as Madam Hartwood's flinty eyes narrow in on my dress.

"My dear, is that ... *magic?*"

She manages to whisper the accusation harshly enough that everyone in the room stops to look at us, the background rumble of voices now gone eerily quiet. The little sparkling silver threads in my dress, which I thought so faint and delicate against the dark green fabric, now seem to blare like spotlights. Cinder rustles encouragingly in my pocket, with a soft squeak. I can feel her warm little body against my leg, steady and still. It gives me a bit of courage, and I straighten up.

"I thought ... just for Yule, just a little bit, that you would like it and ..." *Allow me—and the rest of us—to actually* do *the magic we were born to do. To trust that the ley lines have recovered.*

Now that her face is glowering before me, somehow making her look larger and more intimidating than usual, I realize it was a stupid, *stupid* idea.

"Do you *realize* the harm your little stunt could have caused?" she says, harsh words and spittle flying from her mouth, her usually placidly reverent face contorted in anger—and possibly fear. "The ley lines need to be *protected*. To *heal*. *Not* to be used for trifles!"

"Yes, Madam Hartwood," I mutter, my clammy hands bunching in the fabric of my skirts. The velvet is soft, the embroidery smooth and cool under my fingers. The threads seem to lean into my skin, as if trying to comfort me.

"You will go home immediately and *burn* that … that *mess*," she snaps, looking over my beautiful dress and scowling.

Mess? It may hold forbidden magic, but it's a gorgeous dress, and I feel like a witchy princess in it. Or I did, until about sixty seconds ago.

The other elders of the coven have gathered around us and are making snide remarks.

"Ivy again? Why am I not surprised?" Temperance Blackthorn whispers, but not so quietly that we can't all hear her.

And why has the music suddenly stopped? My heart is pounding so hard that I wonder briefly if I'm going to black out. My breath comes quickly, and contemptuous faces begin to spin around me, like I'm on a vicious merry-go-round.

"Hideous and vulgar," Agatha Carrow comments with a sneer.

"An insult to her parents' memory," a third says. I can't see who.

It is this last comment that sends me over the edge. *My parents would have* loved *this dress*, I want to say, memories of my childhood, spent swirling around in my mother's fancy clothes, dancing like visions in front of me.

I don't give them the satisfaction of seeing me cry. I shoot an apologetic glance at Stella, then turn and flee the festive home as quickly as I can, running out the door like Cinderella from the ball, my embroidered flats slipping on the newly fallen snow. I think I hear Stella call for me once, but then I start running faster. I slip a few more times and gain what is going to be an impressive goose egg on my right knee, and then I can think of nothing except the burning in my lungs and the nip of snowflakes on my exposed skin until I make it to Main Street and up the flight of stairs to my apartment. I've left my coat at Stella's, I belatedly realize, but it's much too late to go back and get it now.

It's not until the door slams and locks, my freezing, burning legs finally giving out, that I slump to the floor and cry, the soggy skirt of my beautiful dress pooling around me, and my brave mouse sitting on my shoulder, pressing her warm little body against my face.

CHAPTER 2

I can't bring myself to burn the dress and release the trace of magic I switched into it. I spent too many hours on it, blurry-eyed after working hours upon hours on the tiny glimmering stitches. Cinder, of course, was a big help, as always. She lit up when I added the drop of magic to the thread, wriggling with excitement. Even now, she looks at it longingly, like she knows as well as I do that *this* is the kind of magic we're meant to make together. Thread magic.

I hang the dress up in my closet instead, behind poofy skirts and corseted tops and silk and chiffon, behind purses and costume jewelry and wigs and wings and shoes upon shoes, until I can barely see it. The silver stars catch the bare overhead light bulb in my closet—a walk-in, of course, the main selling point of this apartment—and the magic is so subtle it's hard to tell if the silver is just glittering or alight with the magic I gave it. *I should have known Madam Hartwood wouldn't like it*, I think, sniffling one last time as I turn and shut off the light.

Now that I'm back in my old *Fairhaven High* sweatshirt, Cinder has claimed her usual spot in the hood. She fusses awhile back there, chirping and squirming until she's comfortable.

I was surprised when Cinder claimed me as my familiar. Honestly, part of me had wondered if I'd even get claimed at all. And if I did, I expected a cat, as most witches have one. Both of my parents did—my mom had a sleek tuxedo cat, and my dad had a fun-loving orange tabby.

But no. I got a mouse.

There was laughter at first, and oh, so many jokes. *Poor Ivy's magic must be confused*, people said. *A mouse! How embarrassing.* I wanted to take Cinder and vanish—but a familiar-claiming party is a big deal, like a bat mitzvah or a quinceañera, so I was required to stay, with my mouse, and my shame.

It didn't take long for me to warm up to Cinder, though. I couldn't have asked for a better familiar, or friend. She's smart, and thoughtful, and so clever with her little paws in ways that a cat never could be. She knows exactly when to cut a thread that I tie off, using her small, sharp teeth. She places sequins and ribbons with expert precision and offers silent advice on everything we create together.

And create we do. Just like Stella's magic is healing magic—not that she ever gets to use it—mine is thread magic. I take one last look in my closet—at the sweater that gives the wearer a fifty percent chance of seeing a rainbow, at the knitted hat that will fix a bad hair day, at the four-inch red heels that are guaranteed not to blister the wearer's feet. And that's besides the costumes I create for my online orders. It warms my heart to think for a moment of little bits of my magic drifting around the world on silk and woolen threads, granting a little smile into each customer's day.

I silently close the door.

I can't sleep. It's Yule, my favorite time of the year. I'm usually giddy from all the decorations and music and smells and sights. And now I've ruined it.

I grab my phone and text an apology to Stella, and tell her that I hope the rest of the evening goes well. She doesn't respond—I don't really expect her to. She's probably too busy with her guests.

But I still wish she would.

I remember when I was little, maybe seven or eight, and the coven was one giant extended family, with dozens of aunts and cousins. That year we had Yule at Hartwood's mansion. It was a little removed from the main roads of Fairhaven, so no one noticed the snowflakes that only fell on her house, or the music played by ghostly instruments, or the punch bowl floating from person to person around the home as if carried by an invisible server. I remember the taste of cinnamon and cranberry on my tongue, the nip of magical snowflakes against my face, the warmth of the roaring fire and of the hugs of my coven, each witch telling me how much I'd grown, what a strong witch I'd be someday, how they couldn't wait to see what magic I'd get. Stella and I used to imagine we had different magics all night, pretending to change Salem from black to gold, or turn the cookie trays into mountains of infinite sweets. We'd pretend we had a unicorn for a familiar, or a dragon, like Thekla the Bold, from *The History of Witches*, a historical book we'd read dozens of times that year.

How things have changed.

Over my kitchen sink, ropes and ropes of white fairy lights twinkle like stars. Across the window behind the sink is my hopeful array of plants—two succulents in chipped teacups, a sprig of lavender in a mason jar, and a small basil plant in a lopsided clay pot Ruby made me for my birthday a few years ago. Basil has its magical uses—happiness spells, mostly. I just think it tastes delicious.

I get my favorite mug down from the overfilled cupboard—like most of my mugs, it was handmade by a local artisan. This one is glazed in blue and cream and says *Witch, please* in wobbling typewriter-style print. I heat some milk in the microwave and mix up hot chocolate with Baileys and a shot of peppermint schnapps. The combination smells sweet and minty and wonderful, like it might embody the entirety of this season, and the tension in my shoulders begins to unknot.

I curl up in my favorite chair in the small living room—an overstuffed velvet piece I found at the local thrift shop. It was probably the star of some 1980s lounge, but for now it's covered in whatever throw pillows I'm most in love with at the moment. Today it's a pair of mismatched star- and moon-shaped pillows that Cinder and I covered in sequins. I settle down between them, throw my mother's favorite old quilt over my lap, and inhale the steam from my drink. Cinder scampers down onto my lap and accepts the small gingerbread mouse cookie I give her—I'd planned to save it for tomorrow, when traditionally she and I open our presents, but tonight we can both use a little comfort. And a little sugar. She nibbles daintily on the cookie after giving it an admiring glance—Marigold, the baker witch down the road, gave the cookie gray icing and glossy black eyes to match my familiar. Cinder seems torn between devouring the sweet treat and admiring it, but eventually her stomach wins out.

Afterward, she sighs contentedly, little gingerbread crumbs neatly picked up by her clever paws. She curls up in the crook of my arm as I read my latest paranormal romance from the library and finish my spiked cocoa.

I take a minute and look out the window of my industrial-style, urban witchy apartment, through the big front window toward Main Street. It's dark now, the lampposts forming little halos of light in the thick snowfall. Strings of red and green and gold lights crisscross the street, and the sounds of carols and laughter drift through the air as gently as the snow.

Snuggled into my chair, cocoa and Cinder and my mother's quilt all around me, watching the snow fall—it might not be the way I planned this evening to go, but honestly, I couldn't possibly feel more content.

A pang of loneliness stabs through me, quickly vanishing. *I'll see Stella and Ruby and Jacque tomorrow*, I tell myself. I've got their gifts all wrapped and ready to go. I even got an entire fruitcake from Marigold for Flossy. *I have friends who love me, and that's enough.*

I drain the rest of my cocoa in a single gulp, coughing a bit as the peppermint schnapps fumes hit my sinuses.

And I'll have to remember to use a little magic next year, even if Madam Hartwood kicks me out again. I'll keep trying until she finally sees that magic doesn't have to be dangerous. It can still be beautiful.

I stroke Cinder's soft gray fur. She stretches under my touch, her whiskers twitching as she moves. Just me and my mouse and the scent of cocoa still in the air.

As long as we have each other, we'll be okay.

"I still say that Santa was a warlock, and Rudolph was his familiar!" Stella says, refilling her wineglass as Ruby finishes tearing open the gifts I brought her—magic-free, of course. I would never want to bring Hartwood's wrath down on this family.

"She says this every year," Jacque says with a wink.

The two of them are cuddled up together on the big white couch in their living room. Flossy is perched on the fireplace mantel, enjoying a piece of the fruitcake I brought her. Stella sticks her tongue out at Jacque, who squeezes her tightly.

Jacque is one of the few humans in Fairhaven who know about witches. We keep ourselves secret—the Salem witch trials were proof enough that humans can't handle having magical folk about—unless a human is deemed trustworthy, a decision that has to be made by the entire coven. When Stella and Jacque were dating, Stella had an Inquisition-style trial with Madam Hartwood presiding, and had to personally vouch for Jacque's ability to keep our secret.

It's not something I've ever had to do, but it sounds awful.

"Auntie Ivy, I *love* it!" Ruby says, pulling out a pink-sequined dress from the mass of wrapping paper surrounding her. It's got a flared skirt, perfect for twirling in. She squeals and holds it up to herself, seeing if it's going to be too big—it's not. The dress is going to fit her perfectly. And not because I used magic, but because Cinder and I are damn good at what we do. Cinder squirms in my hand and climbs up to my shoulder.

"I want to wear it right now!" Ruby says, and she takes off to another room to change, a trail of wrapping paper stuck to her foot following her from the room.

"Quick, open your present while we have a moment of peace," Stella says, giggling.

I look down at the gift in my hands, elegantly wrapped in white paper with a gold ribbon in an elaborate bow that I'm sure Stella did herself. I peel back the ribbon gently.

"It's not another toothbrush, is it?" I ask. "Or a hamster ball?" Cinder was not a fan.

"Open it!" Stella says cryptically.

Inside is a large vintage embroidery hoop that smells faintly of cedar. I breathe in the aroma—healing magic. Stella sometimes, allegedly, uses her magic to help her patients—whenever Hartwood isn't looking, of course—but her magic can be used to heal things besides cavities. I can't tell if the magic seeping from the cedar hoop is hers or someone else's, but it's definitely there.

"I found it on eBay!" Stella says proudly, nearly spilling her wine. "Anything you make with it should have a healing charm embedded in it because of the cedarwood. It's old, of course, and probably not that powerful. But I thought you'd like it."

Tears cloud my eyes. It's just so *thoughtful*, so *Stella* of her. Madam Hartwood might have the rest of the coven convinced that magic is dangerous and the ley lines are unstable, and that any use of magic could basically blow our entire county up, but some of us ...

"I love it," I choke out, and give her a watery smile. I'd tackle her in a hug if she wasn't holding a glass of red wine on her white couch. Jacque, who is a little bit of a neat freak, would never forgive me. As it is, he's watching Cinder make a little nest out of wrapping paper on the floor with pained tolerance. I promise to clean it up before we leave, which seems to relieve him. Cinder shoots me a wide-eyed look, so I have to promise instead we'll take it with us. She rustles happily in her paper and ribbon, like a kid in a pillow fort, occasionally poking out her little nose and bright eyes to see what we're up to. Her belly is round and happy from all the treats Jacque has been sneaking her when he thinks I'm not looking.

"Auntie Ivy, look!" Ruby shouts, coming in and twirling. She has her mother's beautiful dark hair, and it flies around her like a cape. Golden light reflects from the sequins as she moves. And yes, I note with professional satisfaction, it fits her perfectly, hitting just below her knees. Her smile is brighter than all the sequins combined, and she tackles me in a Stella-style hug. My heart is so full—and my stomach, from Jacque's cooking—I feel it might just burst.

CHAPTER 3

It always feels strange to be at work the morning after spending my holiday with Stella, Jacque, and Ruby, when most other people are still celebrating—or recovering—but it's a strangely profitable time for me. I play with the embroidery hoop Stella gave me while I wait for customers. It's pretty, but as I try a few poinsettia flowers out on the corner of an old cloth napkin, I realize that any magic left in the hoop is barely detectable, like a hint of smoke in the air where there should be a blaze. I sigh and set it aside. It's a thoughtful gift, anyway. And Cinder likes it better than the hamster ball from last year.

After the holidays, lots of people bring me their well-intended but ill-fitting clothing gifts for me to alter. Between alterations, repairs, and my online cosplay shop, I stay very busy, especially after a famous actress carried my crystal orb clutch at the Met Gala and it went viral. My fingers are calloused and sore from all the orders I've filled since that day, and the mail carrier probably hates me—all the epoxy, metal fittings, and LED lights are *heavy*—but it makes my crafty heart happy.

And so I knit Fred, the mail carrier, a pair of gloves and a hat every year as a thank-you. If he's suspicious at all about how disproportionately warm they keep him, he's never let on.

Then, like I've summoned them with an unspoken spell, the front door opens, and the little bells above it jingle.

"Welcome to the Golden Spindle. How can I help you?" I say automatically.

"Hello, Ivy, dear. Can you give me a hand—oops!" Iris Lane stumbles and falls to her knees as she approaches my counter, sending an armload of clothing across the old wooden floor.

"Are you okay?" I ask, taking her hand and helping her up.

She fixes her glasses, which have fallen down her nose, and pats the messy bun of bright red hair on her head. I've always liked Iris. She's got a natural maternal vibe that makes everyone want to hug her.

"Oh," she says, a little frazzled. "I'm so sorry. I've made such a mess."

"It's no problem," I say as we gather the items.

We talk over the alterations. There are a few pairs of boys' pants she needs let out—River, her son, has grown another two inches—two dresses that her daughter refuses to wear unless I add pockets to them —little Peony is hard not to love—and a sweater her husband bought her.

"It's far too big, but he lost the receipt, and I can't return it," she says, holding the magenta knit up to her chest. It comes nearly to her knees, swamping the petite woman.

"And the color—I love the man, but really, have you ever seen me wear this color? Can you do something with it, Ivy?" she asks, eyes wide with hope that I can save her husband's poor choice of holiday gift.

"I'm sure I can," I say, examining the fabric. I'm thinking I can remove some of the width and make it a little longer. "How about a sweaterdress? And I'll dye it navy." I'm already reaching for my nearest measuring tape, of which I have about fifty. They're stacked on a narrow shelf along the wall, along with hooks for orders ready to be picked up and a framed piece of cloth elaborately embroidered with a specific date —about which no one asks if they have an ounce of common sense.

"Oh, yes!" she says, a relieved smile on her face. "That would be perfect. You're magic with this kind of thing, I swear." She winks.

"I'll give you a call when it's all ready," I say, folding River's pants. "I can have it all done by tomorrow except for the sweater."

"That's perfect. Thank you," she says.

The phone in her purse rings, and she smiles when she sees who's calling.

"It's Dahlia," she says, showing me the screen. It displays a picture of her older daughter, with short, spiky hair and a nose ring, holding up a calico cat who's wearing a black pointed witch hat and looking less than amused. I made the hat for her for Halloween last year, and she puts it on her familiar at every opportunity. Hecate, the cat, has tried to shred it, bite it, and bury it on several occasions, but I added a charm that made the hat practically indestructible, much to her chagrin and Dahlia's delight—Dahlia knows about the charm, and we pinkie-promised never to tell Hartwood about it.

"She told me to tell you hi," Iris says. "And that she's made another app she's going to have you try out."

Dahlia's magic has manifested in some very interesting, very modern ways. Though only just out of high school, she's taken around a hundred online college courses in computer science and programming. She's a whiz with fixing anything electronic, from cell phones to Roombas, and has a side hustle making mobile apps and selling them to startup companies. The rumor around town is that she is doing very well financially, though she continues to favor her simple black turtleneck and jeans, and she carries an old, beat-up backpack overstuffed with all her current projects.

"Happy to try it out," I say instinctively, giving Iris a wave and a grin as she leaves the store.

The last app Dahlia made was a plant identification app, mostly intended to prevent modern foragers from poisoning themselves. Apparently, foraging—once a mainstay of survival—is now a kind of game for adventurous eaters. The app also lists the uses for each plant, which makes searching for spell herbs much easier, so I actually kept the app once I was done with her trial period. I think Dahlia is also working on a digital grimoire repository with Hawthorne College, in Boston, where all witches can upload their spells and pool their knowledge. Once upon a time, I dreamed of attending the witch college. Those dreams went up in smoke years ago, though, along with so many others.

Cinder, who's been napping on a shelf under the counter, scurries up, interrupting my gloomy reverie of academia. She investigates the garments on the table, wrinkling her nose in obvious distaste at the sweater.

"I know. We're going to fix it," I say.

Cinder runs her agile paws over the hem of the nearest pair of pants, looking up at me inquisitively.

"Yes, River must be going through another growth spurt. He'll need these let out again before Ruby's familiar claiming, probably," I say, looking at the pants.

Warlocks, or male witches, are rarer than females, for no reason anyone has ever mentioned. Most of us end up marrying humans, like Stella. My own modest forays into the world of witchy dating have been disastrous. I have never met a warlock who isn't insufferable—besides River, but he is only nine—and have never met any humans who I think I'd be able to trust with my secret.

So for now, it's just me and Cinder. I'm grateful that familiars live as long as their companions—barring some tragic accident, like the time Salem nearly *ate* Cinder. I can't imagine a world without her. I give her a fond pat, and we get to work.

I close up shop around three. No one besides Iris has come in, and the snow is falling harder. I can't see why anyone would be out in this mess, except for the boys having snowball fights in the street, using the cars for cover. I bag Iris's sweaterdress, and Cinder and I head upstairs to our apartment. I bought the two-story apartment and store on Main Street when my parents died. I sold our home on the east side of town a few years ago and used the money to buy this place.

I couldn't stand to stay in our home any longer after the accident. I'd really been living with Stella's parents until I turned eighteen. Stella and Jacque married young and moved out. I think Stella's mom especially was glad to have someone to keep them from being true empty nesters for a while longer. And even after that, I spent more nights there than I ever did at "home," until Stella's parents moved to Arizona. It took years—and some serious therapy—before I was ready to face selling my childhood home.

So, up the narrow brick stair we go. I drop my purse and keys off in the kitchen and head for my workroom—the apartment's second bedroom. Most of the clothing alterations I handle downstairs, and the rest I bring up and finish here. It does make a work–life balance tricky, but it's not like I have much of a social life, anyway, outside of Stella and her family. Besides, I *love* my apartment. It's all exposed brick, and my decorative touches have given it a certain industrial-witchy-chic aesthetic.

I swing open the door to the workroom. Mannequins and dress forms huddle in one corner, a half-finished dress commission glittering like stars in another. On my table, a strewn assortment of scissors, pincushions, and half-finished cups of tea. My workhorse, a black Singer Featherweight 221 sewing machine, sits in the middle of the table. I run a finger over it affectionately, wishing I could sit and play with it. On a small table in the back of the room, under the window, where it catches the light, is my grandmother's old Singer sewing machine from the 1930s. It's a gorgeous old model with a wrought-iron treadle and swirls of chipped gold and red paint along the sides. It still works, but it's an antique, and I'd never forgive myself if I broke it.

Beside my grandmother's Singer is a woven basket full of knitting needles in traditional steel and bamboo, but also iron, rowan for protection, birch for baby clothes and blankets, and even bone. I've never used those, but I can't bear to give them away.

Next to the needles are plastic bins full of colorful yarns—wool, but also silk, cotton, and linen, along with a drop spindle and some supersoft lambswool I've yet to get around to spinning into yarn—and an antique wooden thread cabinet stuffed with years of my thread collection, including my pride and joy, a small spool of shining white thread made from the tail of a unicorn.

On the other wall, shelves full of buttons—metal, wood, antler, and bone. No plastic—magic won't stick to it, and honestly, I just don't like them. There are also ribbons, bolts of fabric, and some gorgeous finely made chain mail I am going to use to make a mithril-style shirt for an online customer. There are no buttons or scraps or anything on the floor, nothing out of place—Cinder doesn't stand for a messy workspace.

There is, however, a petite ghost hovering over my worktable, tsking to herself as she reviews my sketches.

"Hello, Granny," I say, moving the sketches to the side and laying out Ivy's sweater.

"Granny" isn't actually my grandmother. She's my grandmother's grandmother's grandmother, or something to that effect. She tells me every so often that she's a ghost because she was one of the witches executed at the trials in Salem, then forgets she's told me and tells me again. Some spell she cast allowed her spirit to live on—not to avenge her death or that of her coven, but to pester the shit out of her descendants, apparently.

Granny wears a plain dress—eerily similar to the one Madam Hartwood wore to the Yule party—and her white hair is eternally pulled back into a soft bun. If she had a familiar when she was living, she doesn't mention them, and there are no ghostly cats or owls around here that I've ever seen. And Granny sometimes disappears for days at a time, but she always comes back. I've asked her why she's bound to me. She says it's because I'm her last living relative, which still makes me cry when I think of it. What happens when I die, inevitably alone and childless? Will Granny be set free? Or will she just … disappear?

"It's a waste of fabric and time, not to mention your talent," Granny huffs, drifting past my mannequins. I grin at her sour attitude. "Plain, serviceable clothing, and sturdy shoes. That's all a girl needs. I never saw such … such frippery in all my days."

I've heard the complaint a thousand times. She especially loathes the bolts of lace, glaring at them as she drifts past. I think secretly she admires them, but since I haven't yet figured out a spell to make fabric … well, into ghost fabric, she's going to have to wait for her lace dress. And I really don't mind having her around. She's like a room-mate, but one who doesn't make a mess in the kitchen. Or pay rent.

I head for the workroom closet—this room was a bedroom first, after all—and turn on the light. Boxes upon boxes are stacked here, in precarious, dusty towers, as far back as I can see. These boxes contain all that's left of my parents, of the sum of their lives. *Dishes*, one box says. *Pictures.* There are several boxes of those.

There's a small box, taped tightly shut, labeled *Egypt* in bold black marker. I know its contents by heart—a fragment of parchment, said to be from the legendary Book of Thoth. A vial of sand, taken from the inside of a pharaoh's tomb. An ancient stone amulet carved into the wedjat eye. There were more—my parents had a bit of an obses-sion with Egypt at the end of their lives—but the more important pieces were with them when they died, and were destroyed.

I remind myself that I need to organize this closet someday, snif-fling slightly—it's the dust—and turn to look over any box I can find labeled *Books*. There are at least a dozen of these—my father was a collector, or "book dragon," as we used to tease him.

Fortunately, the box I am looking for is right at the top. It's been a few years since I last pulled it out—I really should keep it out in my workroom, but for so long the grief was just … too fresh. This book belonged to my grandmother—not Granny but my father's mother. My dad used to tell me I got my thread witch magic from her. I would like to have known her, to have learned from her. As it is, my spells are limited to what I can find in their old grimoires and my own meager experimentation.

1001 Spells for the Thread Witch is a tattered leather-bound volume, the pages as yellowed and dry as fall leaves. Some of the pages have been dog-eared many times. I flip toward the back, to the spell that will help me move the excess fabric of Iris's sweater seamlessly—pun intended—to the bottom. The color I can handle the old-fashioned way, with dye, so I'm not worried about that part. I'm already running through the plan in my head when I turn, and my hip catches the box of books. They spill out across the room in a big, messy pile. Cinder squeaks in surprise from her perch on my shoulder, then sneezes as the cloud of dust reaches us.

"Sorry," I mutter—to Cinder and to the books. They don't deserve to be kept in dusty boxes in a closet, never to be read or shared. Some of the tomes are gorgeous, ancient family heirlooms and grimoires with tooled leather covers. I've read most of them, though since my magic and theirs mostly aren't compatible, they're not of much use to me.

But if Madam Hartwood ever stopped by and saw them on my shelves? Even if I wasn't using them, she'd have them confiscated and probably destroyed, to keep any curious young—or youngish—witches from attempting spells that could further disrupt the town's ley lines.

So in the boxes they stay.

Granny eyes the books on the floor with interest.

"My great-granddaughter wrote this one," she says, floating over a somber black volume.

I open the cover absently as I gather the books—*Winthrop Family Grimoire* is written on the first page in faded script. I wonder what spells she wrote down, what was important to her to keep, to make sure they got passed on to the next generation of Winthrop witches.

No, I tell myself. *Wondering doesn't get you anywhere.*

I put the books away and carefully shut the closet door. It feels like I'm trapping something inside, something yearning to be set free.

I square my shoulders and flip open the book to find the spell on moving fabric. I set out Iris's sweater and begin.

Most spells are pretty straightforward, at least the ones I use. There's some incantation, usually in rhyme. Sometimes there's a potion or poultice with various herbs or other ingredients, which, honestly, I get mostly at the grocery store down the road and rarely because I've actually foraged for them. The rocks and crystals I keep in a small chest, inherited from my mother and some gifted from Stella, to be used when needed and kept locked under my bed otherwise. There is a chest for the tools there too: mortar and pestle, a knife—I know from personal experience that I can't just use my butter knives to cut herbs for a spell, as it makes it go all wonky—incense, and candles. These last ones I use as sparingly as possible—I have no idea where to get more. It used to be the witches of Fairhaven all shared ingredients and knowledge. I've even looked on eBay, and I can't find these candles anywhere.

Fortunately, for the sweater conversion, I just need the right incantation. I speak the words, and the knitted fabric shimmers like water. The extra material in the sides flows down to the bottom, adding inches of length and a neat border.

I close the book, looking at the dress, and hold my breath a moment.

But the world doesn't end. The ley lines don't go crazy—at least, I don't think they do. I feel sure that if the magic in our town had completely vanished, I'd feel *something*, at least. Like maybe an earth-quake, or at least an ominous clap of thunder.

But the only sound I hear is Granny's sniff of disapproval, and Cinder's squeak of encouragement. I hold up the dress, admiring it from several angles. It looks right. I grab a tape measure and double-check the dimensions, but as usual, the magic is perfect. I set the dress in a tub of warm water to prepare for the dyeing process.

As it soaks, I eye the unfinished dress on the mannequin in the corner. A very exacting customer ordered this from me from my online shop. If every stitch isn't perfect, she'll leave a scathing video review that will likely go viral—she's done it before. Which is why I even offered to accept this order from her, when all I wanted to do was refuse it. It's a chance to set things right.

So I get out my thread and pincushion—and a small iron cauldron full of sequins—and Cinder and I get to work.

CHAPTER 4

The next day, as foretold, Dahlia comes by my shop.

I've always liked her. She's cool in a way I'll never be, with spiky hair and lots of piercings and an infinite supply of big boots. She always wears black, but in an ironic, beatnik kind of way, not really in a witchy way. Not to say she isn't an excellent witch, because she is. Or would be, if Hartwood ever let us try magic beyond Dahlia's tarot card reading and apps, which are walking a fine line, to be honest. I once asked Hartwood if it was all right for me to sprinkle salt across the thresholds of my apartment and hang a rosemary bundle above the door for protection. She stared at me like I'd suddenly grown horns. All magic, not just the spoken spells, was banned.

Stella asked her if this included margaritas with their protective rim of salt, citrus for clarity, and tequila for courage. Hartwood's look of complete bewilderment is something I will treasure forever. Later, our "book club" determined that margaritas were, in fact, allowed … though we never technically ran this by Hartwood.

"Hi, Ivy. I'm here to get my mom's stuff. I can't believe you're done already," Dahlia says.

What I hear is *Don't you have anything to do over the holidays except work?* I plaster on a smile and hand her a bag with most of the garments inside.

"Tell her to give me a few more days on the sweater. The dye takes a while," I tell her.

Dahlia nods and hands me some rumpled bills that I'm sure Iris gave her. Dahlia doesn't believe in paper money anymore. She likes to use her phone to pay for things, and even talked me into getting a tap-to-pay dock at my cash register.

"Your mom mentioned you're working on a new phone app," I say, making small talk while I wait for her receipt to print.

Dahlia lights up. "Oh yeah! You should check it out. It's perfect for you," she says, pulling out her phone and tapping a few times. A red screen pops up.

Heartline, it says.

My stomach drops. *Great.* It's another dating app. Not like I haven't already tried all of them.

The title dissolves into a diagram of a hand with lines crisscrossing the palm.

"What kind of app is this?" I ask.

Dahlia bounces on the balls of her feet, leaning over the counter to show me.

"It's an app for palmistry!" she says excitedly. "You scan a picture of your palm, and it does a reading for you. It's like a dating app, but for witches!"

"So … you have to be a witch to sign up? How do you know who's a witch and who's not?" I ask, handing her phone back gingerly, like it's going to bite me.

She gestures impatiently for *my* phone, which I reluctantly pull out of my pants pocket and hand to her.

"Well, they might have a mystic cross, for example, or we could match the mount of Apollo," Dahlia says, typing away on my phone.

These words mean little to me. I have no tarot or palm-reading magic, though I vaguely recall seeing a book about them in one of my family's boxes yesterday.

"So you're using magic … in an app?" I ask, eyebrow raised.

Dahlia goes pale, and I realize I sound accusatory, like the rest of the town.

"Oh, no, no magic," she says quickly, handing my phone back. "Just basic palm-reading. Anyone can do it. You can even Google it. I just designed an algorithm to do it for me, and to set you up with your soulmate."

"Soulmate," I deadpan, looking down at the little red heart icon on my phone. It seems glaringly out of place there.

"Using palmistry to find your one true love has to be better than hitting the local bars and coffee shops. I should know," Dahlia says, sighing.

We reflexively look through my storefront at Song's coffee shop across the street, known for its "jet fuel" across several counties at least. A blond man with a golden retriever enters the shop, which isn't too busy today. Animals are well tolerated in our town, not least because of all the witches' familiars, even if the humans just think we're eccentric women who love their pets. Well, the cats are welcomed, mostly. Mice? Even the most well-behaved and beautiful mouse can still draw prejudice, so Cinder ends up staying in my pockets most of the time.

"On that note, I need some coffee," Dahlia says, eyeing Stillwater Coffee with interest. She's practically vibrating with energy already, so I suspect it won't be her first—or even third—cup today.

"Eat something too," I remind her.

She waves a hand dismissively, grabs her mother's bag off the counter, and shouts a goodbye as she heads across the street.

That night, as I prepare another batch of epoxy for my "famous" orb purses, I eat a dinner of leftover bread and cheese from Jacque and Stella's holiday dinner. Add in a glass of cheap red wine and some fruit from the fridge, and it's my very own charcuterie board.

Well, mine and Cinder's. I set aside a little plate for her too. She has quite the discerning palate for a mouse.

While I mix the epoxy and eat my dinner, my eyes keep wandering back to my phone, sitting oh so innocently on the worktable.

I got an email earlier in the day that said *Congratulations! You've been signed up as a beta tester for Heartline!*

Dahlia, I cursed under my breath. How did she get my email address, anyway?

Finish your setup now! Scan your palm, and be connected to your soulmate!

I waver, considering. The odds that anyone who Dahlia has given this app to will be my "one true love," as she put it, are slim. And like with her past projects, she probably needs every single participant to help her work out the bugs in the app. So it would really be quite rude of me *not* to participate, to help out a friend. And really, what do I have to lose?

My decision is made. I snatch up the phone, startling Granny in the process, and hold up my palm in front of the camera.

"What in the goddess's name are you *doing?*" Granny shrieks, one hand on her translucent chest.

"Learning palmistry," I say wryly.

The app takes a picture of my hand and highlights the three major lines—life, head, heart—and many more minor lines. It turns out I *do* have a mystic cross, or an x-shaped mark between my head and heart lines, which is common in witches, according to Dahlia. The app congratulates me on this rare mark, which is associated with increased intuition and a "connection to the unknown."

Magic isn't unknown, just forbidden, I think grumpily.

The app offers to read the other lines for me, but I ignore those for now.

Okay, so I have a mark on my palm that may or may not be associated with being a witch. Fine. And this app is going to connect me to a warlock who also matches my heart line? An exceedingly *rare* warlock? I know every warlock in this town, and if I "match" with a single one, I vow I will send Dahlia a scathing review.

"Palm reading? My dear, you need a *real* witch for that, not some ... some app!" Granny says indignantly.

Her comment goes "in one ear and out the other," as my mom used to say. I hold my breath as I wait for the app to tell me it has found my Prince Charming, and whether he is Chad, the warlock a town over, with garlic breath, who told me he wanted to date me because I "came from strong magic genes" that he wanted his offspring to inherit. *Ew.*

The app informs me after a few more seconds that it is still analyzing my lines and finding my matches, and to check back later, so I go back to my wine and cheese. I take the cheddar. The little wheel of Brie is for Cinder. We split the grapes.

And I definitely do not check the app every few minutes to see if it's working yet.

The next morning, I awake not to my alarm but to Cinder's cold nose against my face and her silky whiskers tickling my cheek.

"Morning," I mumble.

She squeaks at me to get up, and as I crack open an eye, I see her scurry over to my phone where it charges on my bedside table.

Congratulations! You have 2 matches! the Heartline app tells me.

"Please don't be Chad," I whisper, pulling up the app. I am now fully awake and run a hand through my hair, pushing the green strands back from my face. For some reason, my heart is pounding.

I open the app and click on *Matches within 50 miles*.

The first is David, a handsome—human—man I've known since grade school.

I wonder if his wife knows he's on a dating app.

I click the *x* with a groan and move on to the next, and last, match.

It shows a man with curly blond hair and glasses, crouched next to a golden retriever who is smiling, with a long tongue lolling out. The dog's, not the man's. Though the man is smiling too, and is quite attractive, honestly.

"Rowan Hale," I read to myself, walking absently toward the bathroom. I frown. He looks familiar. I think I must know him from somewhere, but I can't place it. I'm pretty sure I don't know anyone named Rowan. It sounds appropriately witchy, though. We do like our nature-themed names.

To view the complete profile, please fill out your own first, the app prompts me.

I frown but click the link. It wants a picture of me, and some basic information—favorite food, dream vacation, favorite quote, interesting facts. I can just imagine how our first conversation might go ...

Hi, Rowan. I'm Ivy. An interesting fact about me is that I have green hair. Like, it grows in green due to a spell I cast as a teenager, and I've never reversed it. Also, I'm a witch with a mouse for a familiar.

I sigh in defeat as I put down my toothbrush. He *is* cute. Really cute, in a clean-cut, Ivy League kind of way. He looks about my age. And he has a dog. I don't know for sure if he's a human or a warlock, but my guess is human. And a human who likes dogs is better than any warlock in this town.

I peel a banana and give a piece to Cinder as I make my morning coffee. My phone sits on the kitchen counter, somehow both silent and judgmental.

"You're not going to get a man by just staring at that thing," Granny says, helpfully, as I pour a substantial amount of peppermint creamer into my cup.

Suddenly she's a fan of the app, I think with a grin.

Then Cinder looks up at me and nods. I pause—it's rare that she and Granny agree on anything, especially when it comes to my love life.

Then I pick up the phone and text Stella.

"I got here as quick as I could!" Stella says, slamming open the door to the Golden Spindle at exactly 12:01. Flossy, looking flustered and squawking loudly, flutters in behind her. "We're on lunch break! Let's do this!" With her dentist's white coat over her impeccable camel skirt and silk shirt, she *definitely* looks out of place in my dark and moody alterations shop.

"You didn't need to come all the way over ..." I start, but Stella brushes off my attempt to stall.

"I have twenty-nine minutes. And I've been thinking about it *all morning*. Come on, show me the app!"

Stella plops down on a stool at my counter, fishing out a paper-wrapped sandwich from her purse, the kind that comes from a fancy sandwich shop, only this one was made by Jacque. I can always tell, because he draws a little heart on the wrapping. Stella opens the sandwich and savors the stack of ingredients he's arranged as I set my phone down between us.

"Oh, he *is* cute!" Stella squeals, spinning the phone around to take a closer look. "Like a clean-cut, nerd-slash-vacations-in-the-Hamptons kind of guy. Totally your type."

I shrug in agreement. She's my best friend for a reason. Sometimes I swear she knows me better than I know myself.

"So, like, should I try to be flirty on this profile? Or just state the facts?" I ask, biting my lip. I've never actually matched with anyone *interesting* on a dating app before and then actually gone out on a date with them. Or even matched anyone *potentially* interesting. And it's got less to do with me having unreasonable standards and more to do with living in a boring small town. And *damn it*, but I want to make a good impression on Mr. Rowan Hale.

"Let's go with … a *little* flirty. We don't want you to sound too boring. Favorite food? How about … champagne and oysters?" Stella says, taking a bite of her sandwich.

"Yuck," I say, stealing my phone back. "I'm going to be truthful on this. For … posterity. And Dahlia."

Stella raises an eyebrow but can't say anything, because her mouth is full of sprouts and avocado.

"So … what, then? Cinnamon bun?" Stella asks.

I nod, typing in my answer.

"Looking for a man like a cinnamon bun," Stella muses. "Hot and sweet."

I grin but type away in the little app.

"Dream vacation?" Stella asks.

"Anywhere," I say. I've barely traveled. "How about … to exotic Connecticut?"

"Ooh," Stella says. "That will *definitely* make him want to tear your clothes off."

"Paris," Granny supplies, materializing upside down and halfway through the ceiling. "Paris is always a good idea."

"I didn't know you'd watched *Sabrina*," Stella says, unfazed by the ghost. She and Granny usually get on well.

"Who?" Granny says.

Stella shakes her head.

"Paris *is* a good idea. Very romantic," I say, typing again.

"The rest is pretty easy. Approximate location, age, height, hair color, occupation. Ooh, favorite quote?"

"Walt Whitman," I say automatically.

"Who?" Granny says again, still upside down and halfway out of my ceiling.

"A little after your time," Stella calls.

Granny huffs and disappears in a puff of white smoke.

"Okay, do you have a picture you're going to use?" Stella asks.

"I was thinking that one you took of us at Yule? I'll crop you out," I add quickly.

Stella nods in agreement. "Yes. You looked superhot that night. Do it," she orders.

I roll my eyes but upload the picture. I *did* look superhot that night, even if Madam Hartwood ordered me to burn the dress—which is still sitting in the back of my closet, perfectly unburned.

"Okay. What do you think?" I ask, handing her the phone.

Stella scrolls down, her dark eyes focused with laser precision. I know she's reading the quote at the bottom. Her eyes flash up to meet mine.

"It's perfect," she says, and hands the phone back. I see she's already hit the *Submit* button—most likely to keep me from chickening out.

I scroll through my profile. It's not bad, I think, and I read the quote at the bottom.

"Keep your face always toward the sunshine, and shadows will fall behind you." Walt Whitman

"I've got ... ten minutes left. Let's check out Rowan's profile," Stella says, scooting her stool closer.

I take a deep breath.

And I click the link.

CHAPTER 5

My first impression of Rowan is … surprisingly positive. Tousled blond hair, little wire-rim glasses, and a button-up shirt with a sweater that make him look like a sexy librarian. His dog, I learn, is named Mabel. She has tousled blond hair too, and the kind of happy smile that golden retrievers always have. I learn that Rowan likes Italian food, and that he wants to visit Cairo someday.

It's his quote, though, that makes a teeny, *tiny* spark flutter in my cold, dark heart—another poet, though apparently he prefers Yeats to Whitman.

The world is full of magical things, patiently waiting for our senses to grow sharper.

I scroll back up and look at the photo again, peering harder at Mabel.

"Do you know any warlocks with a golden retriever familiar?" I ask. The quote he chose has me … wondering. He could just be trying to be clever, to cultivate a bookish, intelligent persona. Or maybe there's something to this palmistry thing after all. There aren't many dogs as familiars, at least not here. A fox, yes, but no dogs since Virtue Goodman and her black Labrador left town a few years ago.

"Nope," Stella says, downing the last of her Diet Coke and getting up from the stool. "Warlock or not, Ivy, give him a chance. Maybe ask him out for dinner." She gestures to the eateries across the street. "Just not tomorrow. Book club!"

"Right," I say, mentally swearing. I have, actually, completely forgotten about that. And it's my turn to host.

Stella is right about Rowan—I *should* at least message him and see what he's like. And if he wants to go out sometime. Well, it's been ages since I've dated anyone, so I might say yes, just so I don't get rusty.

Stella is still staring at me with a goofy smile, and I swear I can see hearts in her eyes. She wants all her friends to have the same kind of happily-ever-after that she and her French-Canadian chef husband have, and I'm not sure that kind of magic exists in Fairhaven anymore —even if I secretly wish it did.

"We're still good for six, right?" Stella asks as she fumbles in her purse for her own phone.

"Right," I repeat, making a mental note to clean up my apartment and pick up some food that isn't ramen or Lucky Charms. Book Club is sacred, after all. No matter what, we never miss our monthly meeting.

Promptly at six o'clock, Stella shows up with a bag carrying three bottles of red wine, Flossy perched neatly on her shoulder—and a plant.

"Consider him a housewarming gift!" she says, grinning around the long, waving vines.

"No," I say firmly, crossing my arms. "And I've been in this apartment for years."

"But Marvin *loves* you!" Stella coos, heaving the wiggling mistletoe at me.

I narrowly avoid dropping him—by reflex. If I'd thought about it, I probably would have let the bastard fall. Long, smooth branches begin to coil around my upper arms, and I thrust him onto the kitchen table before he can really latch on.

"You could use more plants here, you know," Marigold says from behind Stella, unable to stop the smile on her face. She has an armload of baked goods that smell *delicious*, which is the only reason that I let her in the door after that comment. Her cat, Biscuit, comes trotting in behind her, fluffy tail held high. She's a Maine Coon, which means she's gigantic and fluffy, like a big, cuddly stuffed animal. Biscuit I adore. Marvin, not so much.

"Did you bring cinnamon buns?" I ask, watching Marvin inch closer to me.

Flossy flutters up to a cabinet, while Biscuit makes herself comfortable on my velvet chair, happily kneading the sequined pillows. I never can tell if she's orange-striped with white patches or if it's just flour from Marigold's Bakery that makes her fur look that way. Regardless, she's never shown the slightest interest in eating Cinder, so she's always welcome here. Plus, she's very cute and quite possibly the second-softest familiar I've ever known, after my own, of course.

"Yes, I brought your cinnamon buns!" Marigold says, beaming. She knows her way around my kitchen—or all kitchens, really, and I have to wonder if that's some weird aspect of her cooking magic—and she begins plating up an assortment of yummy treats. Marvin wiggles happily when she strokes one of his leaves, and I try not to roll my eyes.

"You really had to bring Marvin? Really? I thought you were my friend," I say accusingly to Stella.

She grins and rifles through my kitchen drawers for a bottle opener.

"Third drawer on the right," Marigold offers helpfully, not even looking. Her blond curls bounce as she skips around the kitchen, and in the blink of an eye, the table is set.

"So I ran into Madam Hartwood at Wicked Wines this evening," Stella says, pouring us three generous glasses.

"Oh?" Marigold prompts. I set out the fruit and cheese I've prepared, setting aside some fruit for Flossy and a little cheese plate for Cinder with a raspberry and a grape on the side. She sits happily on the little breakfast bar while we crowd the table with bottles and treats.

"She wanted to tell me all about some nephew who's going to be visiting for a while this year," Stella says, rolling her eyes. "The way she tells it, he looks like a young Brad Pitt and has the brains of Einstein and more magic than Merlin."

"Aw, how nice!" Marigold says with a smile. Then she stops short when she realizes Stella is being sarcastic. She flushes and takes a bite of baguette to keep herself from saying any more.

"Hartwood invited me over for dinner to meet him," Stella says. "I guess she's having some kind of witchy party tonight—she never invites Jacque, you know—but I told her I had book club this evening."

I roll my eyes at Hartwood's snobbery. *I* wasn't invited—and by the look on Marigold's face, she wasn't either. *Typical.* Stella is apparently somehow still in Hartwood's good graces, though I know her association with me makes that tenuous.

"Jacque can come to book club anytime, if you want," I offer, and I mean it. He's practically family, and I trust him not to give us away.

Stella gives me a smile. "I know," she says warmly. Then she slaps a hand on the table as something occurs to her. "Oh, do you know that old crone asked what book we're reading this month?"

"What did you tell her?" I ask, sipping on my wine.

"*The Mists of Avalon,*" she says with a sly smile.

I nearly choke.

"I'll Google the summary so I can be prepared in case she asks any questions," Marigold says solemnly, slipping another raspberry to Cinder.

"On that note …" I say. I push back from the table and head to my craft room closet. There, in the top box, barely covered, is an old book with thick yellowed pages and a black leather cover. I retrieve it with the same solemnity with which I'd carry Merlin's own wand, and place it on the table. "Let's get this book club started."

Stella and I have been meeting once a month for years. It started as our monthly wine night, which—after a few too many one evening— somehow became "book club."

Except the only books we ever read are our grimoires.

After "the accident," Hartwood gathered up all the grimoires she could find. "For safekeeping," she said. I, for one, never believed her. Neither did Stella.

And neither, apparently, did Marigold. Stella and I stopped by her bakery one evening on our way to my old apartment for our monthly magical chat. We don't ever speak of magic in public, of course. That is much too dangerous, and was even before the accident. We can't risk a human knowing about us, and we don't know which witches are spies for Hartwood. As the coven has shrunk over the years as witches have moved away, our list of allies has grown shorter and shorter.

"One cinnamon bun and one chocolate éclair, please," I said to Marigold.

She smiled and rapidly wrapped our purchases.

"Would you two do me a favor and try these for me?" Marigold said, handing us each a shortbread cookie decorated with pale green icing.

She is always experimenting with flavors—and they are always spectacular. Cooking magic is a very nice kind of magic to have, I've decided.

"What are they?" Stella said, already biting into one and fluttering her eyelashes in bliss.

"Lavender matcha shortbreads," Marigold said, her cheeks turning pink.

I bit into my cookie and tasted the familiar tingle of magic on my tongue. My eyes shot to Marigold's, and she turned even pinker.

"Delicious," I said—and it was. The shortbread practically melted in my mouth, and the lavender with the delicate matcha icing? Heavenly. A warmth spread through me, a feeling of just … peace. Like the tight knot of tension always at the base of my neck had suddenly vanished.

Stella and I exchanged a glance. For Marigold to use magic in her baking after Hartwood had expressly forbidden it, and for her to take a chance and trust us not to betray her? Well. Sweet little Marigold had a hidden backbone of solid steel.

"Would you like to join our book club?" Stella asked immediately.

Marigold agreed with a relieved sigh and a nervous laugh.

And this month, it's my turn to pull out my family's grimoire.

"Okay, so this month I tried tying a healing spell into a hat," I say, flipping to the last page. "I used natural undyed wool fibers and knitted Celtic knots into the pattern that I found online." I've only ever tried small magics, like this one. And this one, at least, turned out nicely. Unlike the time I tried to spell my laundry to fold itself, and ended up with every item in my wardrobe *un*folded instead.

And my nice underwear flew out the window like lacey little swans. I miss them.

"What kind of healing?" Marigold asks, helping herself to another piece of cheese—Gouda.

Cinder squeaks in approval, her belly round and happy. She scurries—slowly—up my sleeve and curls up on my shoulder to watch us.

"Headaches, head colds, that kind of thing, hopefully," I say, showing them both the hat.

They turn it over appreciatively, admiring the stitchwork. Knitting isn't my strongest suit, but as a thread witch, I can manage it. I even added a pom-pom on top. Not for any magical reason, just because it's cute.

Stella finishes off her glass of wine and gets up to open a second bottle. Flossy flies down to perch on her shoulder, her long tail-feathers looking like an exotic accessory against Stella's neutral-toned outfit. Stella opens the next bottle with more force than needed, and a little splashes out. She grumbles softly. Marvin hands her a napkin and helps her wipe it up. At least he's a considerate sentient plant. Who definitely is *not* going to live here permanently and is going to go home with Stella *tonight*.

"Are you okay?" Marigold asks Stella softly. She's still glaring down at the place where the wine spilled, though it's all clean now.

"I just … I just wish that *old bat* would let us do *real* magic, instead of us sneaking around like this!" she says.

I sigh and close my grimoire. Usually we get through at least the second bottle of wine before we have this discussion.

"Old bat! Old bat!" Flossy agrees.

Stella gives the parrot a grape, and Flossy flies back up to her perch on my cabinet, where she can watch us all—including Biscuit, who eyes her with interest.

I crumple the hat in my hands. "This *is* real magic," I say softly, ashamed.

Before the accident, my mother could stop storms in their tracks, make rainbows appear on a whim, make sure that every Yule, we had the most delightful sparkling snowfall. And we would *laugh*, and throw snowballs that turned into birds and butterflies, and dance in the rain that somehow never got our shoes and socks wet.

So my hat isn't a rainbow. So no one will ever have beautiful memories of my stupid hat. It is still *magic*. And contrary to what Hartwood thinks, the ley lines haven't collapsed. In fact, there have been no consequences at all. That is as much a part of each experiment as the outcome.

"I think your hat is beautiful," Marigold says gently, putting a hand on my arm. "It is a work of art, *and* you are trying to ease someone's pain with it. That's real magic if I ever saw it."

Stella mumbles an agreement and refills our wineglasses.

"To real magic," I say, lifting my glass in toast, though my words are trembling a little.

"To real friends," Marigold says confidently.

"To someday proving that old bat wrong," Stella finishes.

"Old bat!" Flossy agrees.

Marvin ruffles his leaves.

We knock our glasses together, cheering. As I drink, I swear in my heart that our little acts of defiance are just the beginning.

CHAPTER 6

Bzzz.

It's early, and I'm not used to being woken up by messages. My eyes are still blurry from sleep as I fumble for my phone, nearly knocking my clock off the nightstand in the process. The red Heartline app appears in the notifications—*You have 1 message.*

Before my sleep-intoxicated brain can think better of it, I click on the app.

Hello.

It's from Rowan Hale, the mysterious stranger that Dahlia's app set me up with based on my palm reading. Supposedly. I really need to get out that palmistry book and take a closer look at what she's up to.

And yet despite my skepticism, I can't deny that my pulse picks up a little at seeing his message. I sit up, brushing strands of green hair back from my eyes. I text back.

Hello.

Hello? It's been a while since I've flirted with anyone, but really, is that the best I can do? I bite my lip, trying to come up with something clever. Rowan beats me to it.

. . .

It seems we have a mutual friend.

I frown.

Who?

Dahlia, the very persuasive and persistent girl who asked me to help with her app.

Oh, yeah. *Duh.* I wince.

So, are you from Fairhaven?

Boston, actually. Just here for a little while visiting family.

Boston. Okay. I wonder if there are any witches I know in Boston who could tell me if this Rowan Hale character is a warlock. I chew on my bottom lip—it's unlikely. Dahlia probably recruited everyone she could to help with her app, magic and nonmagic, just like last time.

Cinder, fur sticking up on one side from sleep, yawns hugely and climbs from her little bed—which is a vintage doll bed—on my nightstand to sit in my lap, then proceeds to straighten her whiskers as she watches me type, erase, and type again. She shoots me a look of exasperation.

I admit I'm not well versed in palmistry, but I promised Dahlia I'd try to help—and honestly, I'm intrigued by your profile. Can I take you out for a cup of coffee? There's a place called Stillwater Coffee I've been to a few times. I hear NASA uses the espresso for rocket fuel.

He's intrigued, hmm? I ponder this. At least he's capable of forming a complete sentence, which is more than some of my past online dating attempts have been capable of.

Sorry if that seems forward—I'm not used to using apps like this.

He must have interpreted my hesitation over finding something clever to say as hesitation about accepting his offer. He's a little unsure of himself, and somehow I find that endearing.

I'm about 95% sure that "rocket fuel" thing is an urban legend. But I love Stillwater Coffee.

Have I screwed up? Should I say that his profile intrigued me too? Or is that just a corny line? The fact that he hasn't already propositioned me or asked me for a nude photo puts him ahead of most of my online dates, so I'm going to be cautiously optimistic.

Do you like dogs?

I grin.

I love dogs.

Dogs rarely try to eat Cinder. Plus, they're cute. All of them, even the squishy-faced ones.

I'd like to bring Mabel with me, if that's okay.

I can't help but wonder if he picked a dog-friendly venue for our meeting—I refuse to call it a date ... yet—because she's his familiar, and we don't feel well when we're separated for too long. Dahlia *did* say this app was designed for witches, though anyone could sign up.

I'm looking forward to meeting her.

And you, I think.

I'm free tomorrow afternoon. Could we meet you there around 2:00?

Sounds great.

I wait, but he doesn't say anything else. I grin. *I'm meeting him for coffee!*

I get up and skip to the bathroom to get ready for the day—texting Stella and Marigold as I go.

I close up my shop early and head upstairs to change for my meeting with Rowan. Marvin is vibrating with delight, his leaves rustling as if a tornado was rushing through my apartment. He follows me like an anxious puppy and leaps happily into my closet to help me pick an outfit. Cinder, perched on my shoulder, lets out a noise that sounds like a little mousy sigh.

I've been contemplating what to wear all day, and how to do my makeup, and what on earth to do with my hair. I don't want to look like I'm wearing a costume, which is how I make my living, after all— the alterations of daily human and witch wear contribute only a small fraction of my income. So I grudgingly set aside the tiaras and ball gowns, the wings and horns and headdresses, and look for something more "normal."

In the end, I settle for a green sweaterdress that matches my hair. It's one of my favorites, because it fits like a dream and has little strands of metallic thread woven through it. I pair it with brown boots, an oversized tan wool coat, and a green version of my "famous" orb purse on a cross-body strap.

The best part of this outfit is the deep pockets in the coat. Cinder can hide in one until I know a little bit more about Mr. Hale, and Song has never minded if she sits on my table and eats a cookie while I drink coffee. Song isn't a witch, just a very animal-friendly human. She doesn't even blink when we come in with mice or parrots or cats. The witches with raven and fox familiars tend to leave them outside, though. The foxes like to steal pastries, and the ravens cause all kinds of havoc, by either opening sugar packets and flinging the sugar around like snow or being a little *too* curious about the humans' wallets.

I walk across the street to Stillwater Coffee, my hair curled and bouncing, and makeup a perfect "no-makeup makeup" look. It's interesting that Rowan has picked this location—he can't know where I live, right? I didn't put my address in anywhere on the app. It is conspicuously convenient, though. Fairhaven is a small town, but even so … I'm pondering this as I enter the coffee shop, the aroma of espresso hitting me like a delicious wave.

"Hey, Ivy!" Song calls from behind the counter. Today her dark hair is tucked back neatly in a tortoiseshell headband, and she's wearing an apron with coffee beans printed on it. "The usual?"

I'm about to respond when someone gets up from the booth behind me and clears his throat.

It's *him*. Rowan Hale. My heart pounds in my chest, and my hands suddenly feel clammy. *Toadstools.* I feel like a teenager with a crush.

"Hi," I manage to squeak. He's quite tall, so even in my boots, I'm looking up at him. Staring up at him. He has blond hair that curls, wire-rimmed glasses, ice-blue eyes, and the nicest smile, which wobbles just a little with uncertainty. He's even cuter in person than in his picture, with straight white teeth and a hint of a dimple on his chin. *Straight teeth? Goddess, Stella's really rubbing off on me.*

"Hi," Rowan says, his face flushing faintly. He shifts his weight from foot to foot, and I realize he's a little anxious too.

I smile back at him—and feel a warm, wiggly weight against my hand.

"And you must be Mabel," I say, stroking the dog's soft back.

Mabel wags with delight, her tail going as fast as a propeller. She appears full-grown, but she's as excited as a puppy, and it takes Rowan a few seconds and a few tries before she calms down and sits neatly at his side, though she's still giving me a lolling golden-retriever smile.

"She likes you," Rowan says, and he grins, like he's relieved.

I shrug, feeling a little self-conscious, and smooth a green curl back behind my ear. In my pocket, Cinder wiggles.

"Most animals do," I say.

"Ivy! Order's up!" Song calls.

Before I can turn, Rowan has paid for my coffee—pumpkin spice is always on the menu here, no matter the time of year—and brought it back to the little blue pleather booth he was sitting at. He hands me the coffee, our fingers just brushing, and gestures toward the seat.

"Join me?" he asks.

I sit, noticing a small bouquet of lavender roses on the table between us, the stems neatly wrapped in brown paper.

"Um, I believe it is customary to bring flowers on a date," he mumbles, rubbing the back of his neck. He's got fair skin—thanks to some Nordic ancestor, probably—and his ears are turning positively crimson.

"For me?" I blink.

"No one's ever brought you flowers?" he asks, a furrow forming between his eyebrows, like he really can't believe this.

Now it's my turn to flush. *Well, he's right.* I think about the bouquets that Jacque always cuts for Stella from their garden—old-fashioned or not, it always feels romantic to me.

"Um, it's just … I honestly can't remember. It's been a while," I say.

He nods, tension leaving his shoulders. "For me too." He folds his hands on the table and whispers, a little conspiratorially. "So, do you have any murderous exes I need to worry about?"

"Nope," I respond. "Just haven't met anyone interesting here in a while. You?"

"No murderous exes," he says. "Just the regular kind. Broke my heart a few years ago, and I haven't felt like dating since."

Goddess, I hope he's not still hung up on his ex. I don't need that kind of emotional baggage. I take a deep breath.

"What changed?" I ask, sipping my coffee. It's perfect, like always, and I hum with delight.

"Well, Dahlia, I guess," he says with a grin. "Did she give you that line about finding your soulmate?"

"She did," I say, blushing. "If, um, you believe in that kind of thing."

"Sure. I guess I'm a romantic at heart. I read a lot," he says in a self-deprecating way, rubbing the back of his neck again.

"I, um, meant the palmistry," I say, and he flushes a deep pink.

"Oh," he says. "Yes. Well, it's an interesting idea, anyway."

We sit in quiet for a moment, not making eye contact.

"So," I say, keeping my eyes on the flowers—which are beautiful—or on my coffee, anywhere but on the piercing, serious eyes looking back at me.

"So," Rowan says, smiling. "I like your hair."

"Thanks. I like yours too," I say automatically, then wince. Before I can stammer an apology, he's laughing again, and Mabel's tail is thumping under the table like a drumbeat. The awkwardness between us seems to have receded a bit, like a curtain being pulled back.

"So, Rowan. What do you do?" I try, cursing my stupid brain.

"I do research for, uh, a school," he says. "Old books and things."

I nod, though he's so vague that I have no idea what he's talking about, and that does make me a little suspicious.

"You?"

"Bespoke clothing and fashion design," I say proudly, looking at my shop across the street. "That's my shop. I do alterations, but also costumes for events and things on my online shop."

"Is that one of yours?" he asks, nodding at my purse.

I hold the green resin orb up proudly. "It is."

He runs a long finger along the chain. He has nice hands. Long fingers. *Nice for palmistry*, I correct myself.

"I've seen a few like it around town. Your work must be popular," he says.

I blush. "A little."

We talk for about half an hour, about mundane things. Work, family, favorite restaurants in town. I keep waiting for him to say something, anything, about whether he's a warlock, but he never slips up.

I wonder, then, if *I* should be the one to say something.

"Um, you said you're visiting family in town?" I say absently, thinking of how I can casually drop *I'm a witch. Are you?* into conversation. Usually I know beforehand if the man I am meeting is magical. Maybe that's what makes Rowan so interesting—the mystery. He's attractive, obviously, but also sweet, and a little shy, and he seems to think *I'm* interesting. *Maybe we'll make it to a second date*, I think as he finishes his coffee. *Maybe ... Italian food.*

"I'm staying with my aunt, Patience Hartwood," Rowan says.

I choke on the last bit of pumpkin spice in my cup, then cough for a minute.

"Hartwood is your *aunt?*" I wheeze, thinking back to book club the other night. Stella *did* mention Madam Hartwood had a handsome magical nephew visiting. Oh, *how* did I not make that connection? *Goddess, I'm an idiot.*

And if Hartwood finds out her nephew is on a date with *me*—okay, I'll call it a date now—she might just break her vow to suppress magic and turn me into a toad. Or worse. My insides shrivel up just thinking about her wrath.

"Oh, you know her?" Rowan asks, voice calm. Suspiciously so.

I narrow my eyes at him.

He raises his eyebrows, surprised at my change in attitude.

"Did she put you up to this?" I ask. Is he her spy? Trying to get on my good side, to get me to slip up so he can report back to her on my illicit activities? My heart rate skyrockets. *I should have known he was too good to be true.*

"Aunt Patience? Up to what?" he asks, a look of genuine confusion on his face.

"This," I say, gesturing around the coffee shop, at the flowers. In my pocket, Cinder stirs, concerned at the volume of my voice.

"My aunt has no bearing on my dating life," Rowan says carefully.

If he's acting, well, he's a good actor. I sputter for a moment, crossing my arms. If Hartwood is his aunt, then he is ... he has to be ...

"You have an interesting name, Ivy," Rowan says, staring down at his empty double espresso, changing the topic, like he can sense my distress, and it's given him an idea about my hidden identity as a witch. "Did you know the ivy plant has been associated with protection and fidelity?"

"I did," I say, my suspicion growing stronger. "It's why my parents chose it for me." I take a deep breath. "And why I changed my hair to green, to match."

"You mean, dyed your hair?"

"No," I say, looking him right in his unblinking, damnably gorgeous blue eyes. "Changed."

I hold my breath.

He sighs, exchanging a glance with Mabel under the table. She rests her head on his knee, looking up at him expectantly. He ruffles her ears, an unspoken conversation happening between them.

Then Mabel comes over to me and begins to sniff my coat pocket —the one, specifically, in which Cinder is hiding. The pocket wiggles at Mabel's approach.

Rowan looks around the coffee shop—there are few people here, and none are paying attention to us, except Song periodically checking in to see how the date is going. Once, she pretended to faint to get me out of an awkward date with Chad—I've returned the favor by patronizing her coffee shop as often as I can ever since.

"So I expect that you have a rather small familiar in your pocket, then?" Rowan asks quietly.

I nod and bring Cinder out to sit on the table. She stands on her hind legs, sniffing the air between us and then looking at the strange warlock, cocking her head to the side.

"It's nice to meet you …" he says, looking up at me.

I realize he's waiting for her name.

"Cinder," I supply.

He grins. "Cinder. Do you like pastries? Song tells me the croissants here are amazing."

He's talking to my mouse. Cinder makes a squeaking sound, whiskers twitching. Rowan meets my astonished gaze, giving me a smile that *almost* makes my suspicious heart melt.

"I'll be right back, then," he says.

I exchange a glance with Cinder, and Mabel, whose nose is resting on my knee now. I contemplate bolting while he's gone—I don't need to drag things out any longer than I already have.

Rowan returns before I can make my escape with not one but three croissants, two of them stuffed with chocolate.

He sets half of the plain one on a napkin and places it in front of Cinder, and the chocolate ones in front of us. The piece of croissant is about twice Cinder's size, and her eyes positively sparkle. *Well, he's won over my mouse.* She immediately digs in to her treat and is lost inside the fluffy layers in a moment, only her tail still visible.

"Unusual friend you have there," Rowan says, eyes crinkling behind his gold-rimmed glasses.

"Yours is too," I say.

Mabel has her head on my knee, staring at me adorably. I scratch her soft ears as we eat. She eyes the extra half croissant sitting on Rowan's plate but doesn't leave me.

"So I take it you and my aunt have … a history," Rowan begins.

I raise an eyebrow. "You could say that. She's not my biggest fan."

Based on Stella's report, they must have a close relationship. I don't want to go bad-mouthing the head of my coven in front of her handsome nephew, who I'm trying to impress … Am I trying to impress him still? *Shoot.*

I really should leave.

"Why's that?" he asks. "Did you hex her morning tea when you were little? Pull on Salem's tail?"

I don't like that he's asking questions, even though he's being silly, a smile twitching the corners of his lips. My fingers go cold. *No. She doesn't like me because my parents nearly blew up the ley lines—and did blow themselves up. And now she's banned us all from using magic to "let the ley lines recover," but I can't help myself, and my friends and I have been subverting her for years now, using small magics when she's not looking.*

"Um, Rowan, thank you. For the coffee. And the croissant," I say, looking at my crumb-covered mouse, who is stuffed to bursting. I get up from the table, scooping my fat mouse and the remains of her treat into my coat pocket. "But I don't want to lead you on. This …" I gesture back and forth between us. "This isn't going to work. I ... hope you enjoy your time in Fairhaven."

I return my mug to Song, avoiding her eyes, and head for the door.

"Wait, please," Rowan says.

I freeze, thinking he means to stop me somehow—forget magic; maybe I should start carrying a Taser—but he only opens the door for me, allowing me to step out.

"Can I walk you home?" he asks, looking at my shop, which is only fifty feet away.

"I'll manage," I say dryly.

He runs a hand through his blond curls. He's so handsome I should have known there was something wrong with him. No one like *him* would ever look at a girl like *me*. I can pretend I'm a successful designer all I want, but the truth is that I'm just a girl playing dress-up, stuck in a town I don't want to be in but can't bear to leave. It's like I'm frozen in place, never changing, never leaving.

"Ivy, did I say something wrong?" he asks, breaking into my grumpy thoughts. He looks genuinely concerned. "I thought we were having a good conversation. I can usually only talk about"—he lowers his voice—"*magical* things with my coworkers. I was ... looking forward to spending more time with you."

My heart flip-flops.

"I'm sorry," I say, and I take a step back. I don't know what else to say. *"Your aunt will kill me if she finds out we went out for coffee"*? And say we *did* end up dating—what then? I'd be spending Beltane with Madam Hartwood instead of Stella? Constantly watching my back? No, thank you.

It figures. I finally meet a man who is considerate and thoughtful, and handsome to boot. And he's related to my nemesis.

"At least take the flowers," he says, holding out the bouquet of lavender roses. They smell lovely, and they *are* in one of my favorite colors. "It was ... really nice meeting you."

I glance up at his face. He's fighting to keep a smile, though he's clearly disappointed. *Argh. I have to leave now, before I don't want to anymore.*

I take the flowers. His fingers brush mine, and as our eyes lock, a tingle goes through me that has nothing to do with magic.

Behind me, I hear shouts, and a man parks his car in front of Song's and gets out, phone pointed into the sky.

Rowan's eyes flicker upward behind me, and his breath catches. I turn.

In the sky above us, in the clear blue, *cloudless* sky, is a massive, brilliant rainbow, stretching all the way across the horizon.

CHAPTER 7

I take the narrow stair to my apartment above the shop, lock the door behind me, and slump into a kitchen chair. Cinder scurries out of my pocket. She stands next to my arm, placing a delicate paw on me, a wordless question in her sharp black eyes. The effect is *slightly* marred by the heavy dusting of croissant crumbs—aka bribes—on her smooth gray coat.

Marvin scuttles over, somehow aware that my latest attempt to shake off spinsterhood has *not* gone well. Instead of pelting me with mistletoe berries, he just sits by my chair, leaning his weight against my leg. It's not awful. In fact, it's soothing. Like having another familiar. He plucks the roses from my hand and shuffles into the kitchen, using his long, flexible branches like hands. He plunks them into a cup of water by the sink and begins rearranging them, fluffing the petals. Marvin turns to me, which is not at all unnerving, and *then* proceeds to pelt me with a single mistletoe berry before returning his attention to the roses.

"I know," I sigh, slipping off my boots and jacket. I toss the berry back at Marvin. "He was *nice*. And he's a warlock. And he's handsome, and … it would never work."

Dahlia and her meddling app. So much for "true love." I never trusted palmistry, anyway.

I curl up in front of my TV and try to put Mr. Hale out of my mind.

News of the rainbow has spread fast. It disappeared in a few minutes, but it's got the town in a tizzy and is all over the local TV stations. Suddenly everyone is an amateur meteorologist. Eventually it gets attributed to a solar flare, like a daytime aurora, but the witchy community knows better, and soon my phone is blowing up with text messages from the coven.

Something's definitely wrong with the magic in Fairhaven—and it's done being subtle about it.

"Do you think someday Mom will let me change my hair, like you did?" Ruby asks. "I'm thinking … red." She's sitting at the little vanity set in her bedroom as I curl her hair. I pin it up with bobby pins that have bedazzled stars on their ends. Her room, like the rest of Stella's home, is done up beautifully, in cream and gold, though Ruby has added her own touches—stickers all over the bedposts, a splotch of red on the carpet—mostly hidden by the bookshelf—from a spilled bottle of nail polish. She also convinced Jacque to paint the walls pink a few years back.

And she might have Stella's natural beauty, but she has a love for makeup and hair products that rivals my own—the vanity is covered in lip gloss, mascara, and a thousand other little bottles and tubes. I take another section of her hair and wrap it around my curling iron, then release it and pin it up to cool.

"You have gorgeous hair," I tell her, and mean it. Soft black hair as straight as these pins, and nearly as hard to curl. It falls like strands of black silk over my hands. Her grandmother—Stella's mother, who died last summer—had the same hair, black as ebony, even into her eighties.

"Yeah, but I could really rock red hair," she says firmly, applying an eye-watering shade of pink lipstick in the mirror.

"You could," I agree. "You'll have to go to Hawthorne College or some other town, though. Unless we find a way to fix the magic here in Fairhaven."

Her face falls. She loves Fairhaven as much as I do.

"I'll go, change my hair, and then come back," she says firmly.

"I like this plan," I tell her.

Ruby beams. I can already imagine her using that against me in the future—*But, Moooom, Auntie Ivy said I could!* And what could I say? Giving my niece everything in the world is my favorite thing to do.

"Are we almost ready, my loves?" Stella says, swooping into Ruby's room with a golden tulle dress. Ruby found the design online; Stella bought the fabric, and then I made it for her.

Ruby squeals and jumps from the chair, grabs the dress, and runs in her pajamas to the bathroom to change.

"When did she get so grown up?" Stella asks, leaning against the doorframe with a misty-eyed expression.

I grin, cleaning up my hair tools. "Where's Jacque?" Usually he's underfoot at times like this, snapping pictures.

"Grilling her poor date downstairs. And I think I might mean that literally," Stella says with a sigh.

Ruby's date to the junior prom is a nice human boy named Shane—she's known him since kindergarten. I'm sure he's shaking in his shoes right now, promising Jacque to be home by ten and not a millisecond later.

Ruby emerges from the bathroom, and if I didn't know any better, I'd swear there had been magic involved. She glows, from the beaming smile on her face to the tips of the rhinestone-studded heels she's wearing.

Stella claps a hand over her mouth, unable to speak.

"Pretty girl! Pretty girl!" Flossy says from her perch on Ruby's headboard. Her words make Stella snort, and then we collapse into a pile of giggles and hugs and maybe a few happy tears, before we hear Jacque calling up that Shane's ready.

Ruby smooths her dress—and I have to agree with Stella: *when* did she grow up?—and sails down the stairs with all the grace and poise of a queen.

CHAPTER 8

Beltane is one of my favorite times of the year. When I was little, my mother and I would weave flower crowns together, adding long ribbons in bright colors that would hang down our backs. The coven would have a bonfire out in Farmer Brown's field. Someone would grill, and we'd stuff ourselves with barbecue and fresh spring strawberries and Beltane punch and honey cakes until we were almost too full to move.

And then—we'd dance. We'd have a maypole, of course, and the youngest in the coven would weave ribbons around it until we were dizzy. We'd spin and spin in our dresses, which were usually in lots of green and beautiful, bright floral prints. At some point, we'd kick off our shoes, and our feet would be green and brown from running in the grass all day. Isolated as we were, we'd cast spells that made carpets of flowers spring from the field. And we'd set a thousand glowing lanterns floating into the sky.

Stella's mother used to enchant the punch when no one was looking. It might turn our hair into—harmless—flames, or make glittering patterns show up on our skin, or grant us tiny pairs of translucent butterfly wings that shimmered in the firelight. Once, we even had some werewolves from the next town over join us. They howled at the moon and played games with us until way past midnight.

Then the accident happened.

Ever since, Beltane has been a somber event. And this year, it seems, will be no different.

Stella, Ruby, and I pull up to the field in Stella's SUV. Jacque, being nonmagical, has stayed home, but he has sent platters of delicious homemade food with us. It's one of the benefits of Stella being married to a chef—she can make a peanut butter and jelly sandwich, but that's about it. We get out and open the trunk. We don't say much —I take a glance around the field. Everyone seems to be in a quiet mood.

Ruby has been sulking the entire trip—apparently, her junior-prom date ditched her about halfway through the dance. She called Stella to pick her up instead of letting Shane's mother take them home. There was a quiet rumor about a bowl of punch being turned over Shane and his rented tuxedo. Stella and I made a secret pact to set a hundred frogs on him, or maybe give him really bad acne or something equally horrendous. We didn't, in the end—though Jacque did hint, in a very not-subtle way that was totally unlike him, that he'd be happy to give the boy food poisoning at the next school bake sale.

Ruby's quietly dour mood, though, turned out to be stronger than any of our attempts to make her laugh.

"Can I give you a hand with that?" a distinctly *male* voice says, just as I am mentally cataloging the ten thousandth horrible thing that could befall young Shane.

I close my eyes, not turning around. *Maybe if I close my eyes, he'll go away.*

"Of *course*," Stella coos loudly, shoving me with her shoulder. She's aware of my disastrous coffee date a few months ago now, although, apparently, she does not share my opinion that I should *not* be seen with the nephew of my nemesis. I crack open an eye only so that I can glare at her. She gives me a wide, innocent smile, cocking her head to the side, and mouths the words *He's coming over!*

Rowan joins me at the back of the SUV. I spare only a single quick glance at him—enough to know he's watching me—and return my attention to the carefully wrapped items in front of me.

"You look nice," he whispers, reaching for the cooler.

Despite myself, heat rises to my cheeks. I dressed carefully for the event, definitely *not* just in case Rowan was going to be here, and altered an old gown of mine. It's a corseted confection with layers of ombré purple. The top is decorated with purple silk flowers and positively complements my hair to perfection. The full gauzy sleeves and off-the-shoulder neckline are my favorite parts. One, because the sleeves make me feel like twirling, like a Celtic druid princess, and two, because my boobs look damn good in it. I've even topped off my loose updo with a crown of ivy. *For protection*, I think.

"Thanks," I say, stealing another glance at him. "You too."

And he does, damn it. He's wearing a blue button-up with the sleeves rolled up and khaki pants. He'd belong in a Martha's Vineyard advertisement, if not for the small crown of oak leaves and hawthorn flowers on his head. He reminds me of a preppy, academic warlock prince.

Mabel is at my side in an instant, nose sniffing at all the wonderful smells coming from Stella's trunk, her tail wagging so hard that her entire backside is moving. Cinder is riding in a specially designed pocket by my hip, though I expect she'll run out and play later, like she usually does. She squeaks a greeting to Mabel, who tries to lick her in response. Cinder dives back into my pocket, and for a moment my gaze and Rowan's catch, both of us trying not to grin.

"If you two are done drooling over each other, I'd like to get the food out before the bonfire," Stella teases, hands on her hips.

Rowan does grin then, hefting the cooler and heading toward the small group gathered by the picnic tables in the field.

"You're right. He is cute," Stella whispers to me, shoving an armload of fresh bread and a basket of strawberries into my hands. "Shame you're determined to hate him."

"Why?" Ruby asks, snatching a strawberry from the basket and popping it into her mouth. She's wearing the pink dress I made her for Yule, and the sequins sparkle as she moves. I tied her hair up with ribbons and braids, like my mom and I used to—I don't care if Beltane isn't the celebration it used to be; I'm going to give Ruby the best experience I possibly can.

"Oh, look, Ruby. They've got the maypole set up. Why don't you go check it out?" I say.

Ruby rolls her eyes, clearly aware that I'm avoiding her question, and sighs as only a teenager can.

But her eyes light up when she sees the ribbons fluttering around the maypole, and she takes off. I don't see any other children here tonight—and what's a Beltane celebration without a crowd of sugar-high kids spinning around with ribbons? My chest aches, though Ruby doesn't appear to mind being alone, and she sorts the hanging ribbons solemnly.

Stella and I start setting out the food, and the flower-embroidered linens, which are my contribution.

"I *do* hate him, you know," I whisper to Stella. "He's probably a spy for Hartwood."

"If you did hate him, you wouldn't have worn *that* dress." Stella smirks, eyeing me up and down.

I open my mouth, but no smart retort comes out. She raises an eyebrow and laughs. The movement makes the crystals in her earrings and necklace sparkle—if I didn't know better, I'd say they were enchanted. But no, that's just Stella's natural effervescence.

"Hartwood says he has word magic. That's why he works at Hawthorne College," Stella tells me. "I hear he's on a sabbatical for the rest of the year."

"That's nice," I say, pretending I don't care.

Word magic—that's interesting. Word witches and warlocks are tasked with guarding the incantations we use, and keeping our history. They're the teachers and academics of the magic world.

"Come on," I say, firmly changing the subject. "Let's get this party started."

It honestly feels less like a party and more like a funeral. Marigold finally joins us at dinner. She wears the Celtic-inspired green gown I made for her last year, with a crown of white daisies.

"You look like the embodiment of spring," I proclaim, giving her a hug.

Biscuit twines around my feet, purring. Mabel comes over, tail wagging, and then Biscuit decides that Marigold's arms are a safer place to be.

Marigold has brought all the best things from her bakery, and we stuff ourselves with honey cakes and traditional oat bannocks, also slathered in honey from Marigold's hives, and iced cookies—notably magic-free, of course.

We gather around the pile of firewood as the sun sets. Dinner was a quiet affair. There's been no Beltane punch, just some store-bought fruit juice and lemonade. Hartwood made some proclamations about thanking the goddess for another year, for her blessing on the bountiful harvests in our fields, and for the gifts she has bestowed on us.

Ruby is the only younger witch and gets antsy during the speech—River and Peony apparently have a cold, so Ruby goes off to play fetch with Mabel, and once she's tired out, she cuddles with Biscuit. The maypole ribbons hang unbraided, the ends drooping sadly in the still air.

"She can't wait to have her own familiar," Stella says, watching Ruby make Biscuit a crown of woven dandelions. The cat endures the behavior with her usual good temper, as long as Ruby keeps Mabel away from her.

"Six more months?" I ask.

Stella nods. "More or less."

At Ruby's next birthday, we'll celebrate her coming-of-age with a big party. And during that day, her familiar will make its appearance.

"I'm sure Flossy can't wait," I say with a smile. Flossy is not as forgiving of Ruby's attentions as Biscuit and Mabel are.

I try—and mostly fail—to ignore Rowan for the entire evening. He's the only warlock here, and the older witches—his aunt's friends—positively fawn over him. He's back in town again for a little while, apparently. He answers their blunt questions tactfully and pleasantly. Not that I notice.

"Stop staring," Stella teases, drawing me with her toward the bonfire. "And help me get this ready."

"It'd be a lot easier with magic," I grumble, helping her arrange the stone circle around the firepit. My full skirts don't make it easy.

Stella, looking crisp and somehow not sweating in her sleek olive jumpsuit, isn't having any problem. She grins. "It'd be a lot easier without that dress too."

"I'll just take it off, then. Would you like that?"

It wouldn't be completely out of character to be naked on Beltane.

I can almost imagine the look of horror on Hartwood's face if I stripped—it might almost be worth getting cast out of the coven.

"Rowan would like it," Stella teases.

I roll my eyes and rake the sand around the firepit. It's not a huge bonfire, not like we used to have. It's barely large enough to roast marshmallows on. But per Hartwood's decree, it would be disrespectful to have a large celebration when the magic is still recovering. I'm so sick of mourning magic that I could scream.

"I would like what?" Rowan asks, coming to help.

Heat floods my face. "Nothing," I say quickly.

Stella gives him a wink, while Rowan just looks confused. Mabel is chasing butterflies across the field, carefree and happy. Supposedly, the character of a familiar is a reflection of the witch or warlock. If so, carefree and playful Rowan isn't a side of him I've seen yet.

For example, Stella and Flossy are a lot alike. Loud, smart, and occasionally obnoxious.

Cinder and I are both small. Hardworking. And a little unexpected.

Marigold and Biscuit are both sweet and adorable and make you want to hug them.

But Mabel and Rowan? Well, it doesn't matter. I don't need to know him better, because we're not happening. Ever.

The witches begin to assemble around the firepit, including Dahlia, who is delighted to see us.

"So, Rowan tells me you two matched on my app! What do you think? I'm onto something with this palmistry matchmaking thing, aren't I?" Tonight she's wearing black again—surprise—but in layers of soft silken strips that move with her like mist. She's added thick black boots with silver buckles, a dozen rings, and thick black eyeliner and mascara.

"I'm ... sorry, Dahlia," I say, glancing at Rowan for a moment. "I think the app could use some work."

"Huh," she says, wrinkling her nose. "That's not what *he* said."

Stella elbows me in the ribs. Marigold fights a laugh. Rowan coughs, suddenly finding his shoes absolutely fascinating.

Madam Hartwood and her biddies approach us and the firepit. Hartwood says some words about protecting magic and respecting it for the awesome power it is—while she looks at me. Then she nods to Temperance, who steps forward to light the fire.

Temperance uses a damn lighter. She struggles to light the dry leaves and twigs shoved into the base of the wood stack, her hand shaking as she crouches beside it. When Stella and I were children, we'd all light the fire together with a spell.

With a rush, the entire stack of wood before us goes up—in towering, roaring emerald flames. Temperance shrieks and falls onto her backside.

Every neck in the coven swivels to me.

"I didn't do anything!" I protest instantly. "Why is it when something happens, you all immediately blame me?"

"Because it's *green*," Hartwood says acerbically, glaring at me, her mouth pinched tight.

My hand flies to my hair. "If I *was* going to cast a spell—and I'm not saying I would—why would I make it the *only color* that you would instantly associate with me? I'm not *that* dumb."

I eye the fire suspiciously. If I had to suspect someone of turning the fire green to implicate me, it would be Hartwood—but she couldn't do it without using the very magic she's sworn to protect. So either she's telling the truth, or she's a terrible hypocrite. I frown, considering.

"I've been with her the whole time," Stella says firmly, stepping to my side. "Ivy didn't do anything."

"Changing the color of the Beltane fire would require a substantial amount of magic," Rowan muses. "A spoken spell, some herbs at the very least. Ivy has used nothing of the sort tonight."

I look up at him in surprise—he's defending me, and in front of his aunt?

Cinder scampers from her pocket up to my shoulder, her little claws scratching slightly on my bare skin. She perches there defiantly, teeth bared, my little mouse ready to attack.

"Rowan, you are a visitor to our coven," Hartwood says, spittle flying from her mouth. "You do not understand the long history this girl has with … with … subterfuge! Her and the rest of her family!"

"That's not true!" I say, and I surge forward. To do what, I'm not sure. Maybe punch Hartwood in the nose. I'm starting to wish I did know a few good hexes.

Stella steps in front of me, pushing Ruby behind her too. Rowan steps up to my other side, along with Marigold. Marigold, the sweetest, bubbliest witch in the coven, is positively glaring daggers at Madam Hartwood.

"I didn't do anything," I say again, feeling braver with my friends beside me. "How can I prove it to you?"

The fire continues to crackle ominously, the emerald flames soaring impossibly high.

"Oh, how noble of you," Hartwood spits. "Let me just whip up a truth-telling potion. And bring further stress to our ley lines, which are *clearly* still in need of recovery."

"I could do a tarot reading," Dahlia offers from the sidelines.

Hartwood sniffs.

Temperance, now recovered from her ungraceful fall, mutters something about tarot not being real magic.

Dahlia gives her a withering look and then comes to stand by Marigold. Iris, her mother—wearing the navy sweaterdress I made, to boot—hesitates but stays with Hartwood.

We're clearly divided now, on either side of the fire. Us and the rest of our coven. It breaks my heart. When I was a child, my coven was like a giant extended family.

Now? It looks like we're at war.

"Rowan, get over here," Hartwood says. "You do not want to be *tainted* by association with this girl."

"She didn't do anything," Rowan reiterates. "You're being unreasonable."

"I'm …?" Hartwood chokes. "For all I know, this girl has given you a … a love potion! Or cast a spell on you!"

I bark out a laugh.

Rowan's hand finds mine, and I'm sure it's the adrenaline and overall absurdity of the situation, or maybe fumes from the magical fire, but I hold on to it tightly. His grip is warm and firm, and it feels like … like being a ship in a storm and finding a lighthouse.

"If Ivy wants to enchant me, she doesn't have to use magic," Rowan says.

At my side, Stella coos in adoration before smacking a hand over her mouth.

"It's the dress!" Marigold whispers, grinning.

"It's the boobs!" Stella adds.

"Her parents blew themselves up trying to perform a spell that I warned them—I *warned* them—not to. Did she tell you that?" Hartwood says.

A hush falls over the coven. Rowan stills beside me. I hold on to his hand even tighter as my own starts to tremble.

"It's *their* fault, her family's fault, that the magic in Fairhaven is fractured! *Her fault!*"

"Stella, I think I'd like to go now," I say, my voice shaking with rage. Rowan's hand in mine is the only reason I'm still standing. Rage like I've never known bubbles up inside me, like a volcano. If I stay, I know I'll say or do something I'm going to regret.

"I'm tired of this party, anyway," Stella says, grabbing Ruby around the shoulders. "Come on."

Ruby is confused but follows. Marigold doesn't hesitate, just grabs Biscuit and comes with us, her green skirt flouncing and nose high in the air. Dahlia is busy arguing with her mom, Iris, but gestures for us to go ahead. She puts her hand to her ear in a sign that says *Call me.*

Rowan walks us to Stella's SUV, hand in mine. The SUV will be too small for him and us and the familiars, but I hate the idea of leaving him with his spiteful aunt.

He opens the car doors for us, fingers gently releasing mine.

"Will you be okay if we leave?" I ask him.

He gives me a small smile. "Will *you* be okay?" he asks. "I can handle my aunt."

"It's … nothing she hasn't said before," I say.

His jaw tightens. He shuts my door, but I roll the window down so we can keep talking. Behind him, the fire still burns green, the other witches clustered together like nervous hens, staring at it from a respectful distance.

Rowan and I stare at each other for a moment. Stella starts the car and clears her throat.

"Thank you. For defending me," I say.

Rowan nods, self-conscious, and pushes his glasses up on his nose.

"Can I … that is, would you mind if I brought you coffee sometime?" he asks. He's watching me carefully, like I might shatter.

"Tomorrow would be nice," Stella calls from the front.

Marigold laughs.

"Tomorrow, then," Rowan agrees.

I open my mouth to protest, or laugh, but Stella starts backing the car up, and Rowan steps back.

As we pull away from the field, I watch him, silhouetted against the green fire, his hands in his pockets.

We watch each other until the trees around the field obscure us, and the night swallows us all.

CHAPTER 9

The next day, I'm tired and grumpy. My face is puffy from lack of sleep, and all the cold water and concealer in the world doesn't fully hide the dark circles under my eyes. Cinder watches me as I carefully apply my makeup this morning, like she's trying to figure out how to help. While I'm brushing out last night's curls into a respectable pony-tail, Cinder runs and pulls a purple silk ribbon from our crafting room.

She's got good taste. I tie a bow in my hair and thank my little mouse.

I wonder all morning if Rowan will actually come by. I keep busy with the simpler alterations in my queue and then work on a custom gauzy, embroidered bridal veil for an online order. Every time the little bell above the front door jingles, my head snaps up.

But it's never him.

I push back an escaped strand of emerald hair from my face. Looking at the color gets me thinking—why *did* the Beltane fire turn green last night? If it wasn't one of us, then … what? Is it another sign of the ley lines still acting up, like the rainbow in the clear blue sky? And *why* was it green, of all colors?

It feels like a warning, directed at me.

While I'm gloomily pondering the ley lines that are apparently plotting my imminent demise, the door opens again.

And in walks Rowan with an armful of goodies from Song's, Mabel wagging her tail behind him.

"Um, have you had lunch yet?" he asks, handing me a brown paper bag. "Song said these were your favorite."

Cinnamon buns. And a pumpkin spice latte. The aromas whirl

around my little shop, and I can't help but breathe them in with a contented sigh.

"She's right," I say. "Marigold makes them every morning and drops them off with Song. I'm surprised she still had any left—usually she sells out early."

Rowan looks sheepish and takes a sip from his own paper coffee cup.

"Um, Marigold may have asked her to hold one for you, just in case I came by," he says.

I'd laugh, but my mouth is full of cinnamon and buttery cream cheese icing and bliss, and all I can do is smile. For some, the combination of cinnamon bun and pumpkin spice might be too much sugar, but for me, it's perfect, any time of the year.

"You should try this," I say, shoving the bun toward Rowan.

He takes the plastic fork and breaks off a piece. His eyes widen as he bites into it, and I can't help but crow with victory.

"See?" I say, stealing the bun back.

"I see," he says, then freezes. "Um, you have a bit of icing ..."

"Where?" I say. *Oh, goddess! I'm making a mess of myself. What is he going to think?* I grab a napkin from the bag and dab at my cheeks.

"Um, there," Rowan says.

I freeze—he leans over, slowly, like he's giving us both time to change our minds—and with one finger, he wipes away a bit of icing from the corner of my mouth. He's staring at it, my mouth, like he's considering something ... and then leans back, casually licking the icing off the tip of his finger.

"Thanks," I mumble, scrubbing the spot with my napkin. *Oh, goddess! Did he really* lick *that icing off his finger?*

I search desperately for a way to change the subject. I clear my throat. "Um, how did things go with your aunt last night?"

He leans back on the stool at the counter, taking another sip of his coffee. Mabel lies down at his feet and promptly goes to sleep.

"About the same as before you left, actually," he says. "She really blames you for the ley lines in Fairhaven being out of control, doesn't she?"

I nod. He *did* defend me in front of her, after all, so I guess I can trust him.

"A little," I say.

"I see," he says. Then he takes a deep breath, like he's about to dive into deep water. "I have a confession to make."

I freeze.

"I'm not just here to visit my aunt."

"Oh?" I say, my heart suddenly racing. What other reason could he possibly have to be here?

"I'm a part of the Salem Concord. Specifically, my job title is assistant occult investigator. The Concord tasked me with coming to Fairhaven to see why, exactly, the ley lines are misbehaving, and why my aunt hasn't yet been able to fix them. Usually I just work with the college, researching books and things."

I don't know much about the Concord. Theoretically, it's the governing body for all witch covens in the United States.

"So you're here to *investigate* your aunt?" I ask, mind reeling.

He nods slowly. "And by extension, you."

"I see," I say, setting down my coffee cup. And not because it's empty—but because my stomach is suddenly nauseated. I pause for a minute, considering if I want to run away or vomit.

"Can I ask you something?" I say.

Rowan nods, I guess relieved that I'm not immediately running away and/or vomiting. "Of course. Anything."

"Did you know who I was before we matched on the Heartline app?" My heart pounds so loudly in my ears it sounds like a drum inside my head. *Silly Ivy. You want to know if he actually likes you, when he's been using you all along.*

"I did," he says, rubbing the back of his neck. "Or rather, I knew your name. It came up in connection with the event that caused the ley lines here to … malfunction. Matching on the Heartline app was … unexpected."

"I see," I say automatically. "So you invited me out for coffee to … what, interrogate me? Get me to lower my defenses, catch me admitting to something unawares because you flirted with me?"

"No, nothing like that," he says quickly. "I'm nowhere near that devious … and, well, can't both be true? That I came here to do research, to interview you, and also found myself intrigued by you?"

"It's a little hard to believe," I say truthfully. *Though I want to believe it.*

"Tell you what," he says, leaning forward, a conspiratorial twinkle in his blue eyes. "Let's make a deal. You know this town better than I do. I need your help investigating the ley lines. You can be … my consultant. Which lets us spend time together. And if you have nothing to hide, as I suspect you don't, then you have nothing to fear from me or the Concord. And I promise, I won't flirt with you again until you ask me to. I promise to be completely professional."

I bite my lip, considering. It's an outrageous proposal. Though I suppose I'm going to be "interviewed," one way or another. Would it be the worst thing to cooperate? I'm desperate to find a solution to the ley line problem in Fairhaven—and maybe Rowan is the key to figuring it out. After all, he's got insight into Hartwood's mind that I'll never have, not to mention resources I can't even imagine.

"I accept," I say.

He extends his hand, and we shake on it. I release his hand quickly and wipe my palm on my pants, because it's suddenly clammy.

"I'd like to start by getting your side of the story," Rowan says.

I open my mouth, but just then, Iris Lane walks in with more of River's too-short pants.

"Oh, are you busy?" Iris says, eyeing us.

I get up too quickly, anxious that she's seeing Rowan with me. I expect she'll report it directly back to Hartwood.

"Nope. He was just leaving," I say, reaching out for her bag of clothing. "More for River?"

"You know it," she says, smiling tightly.

I haven't forgotten that last night at the green fire, she sided with Hartwood. It hurts, like a knife in my gut. I'd thought she was more than just a customer. I'd thought—incorrectly, apparently—that we might be friends. At least Dahlia seems to be somewhat on my side. I remind myself to call her later.

"I can come back later," Rowan says. He grabs an old receipt and the pen from my desk, scribbles something down, and hands it to me —his phone number.

I wave him off, smiling brightly at Iris. He and Mabel leave the shop without another word.

I don't text him that afternoon. Instead, after I close up the Golden Spindle for the night, I head upstairs to my craft room. Cinder and I spend a few more hours lining my resin orb purses and attaching the chain straps, fulfilling orders and wrapping them neatly in cardboard boxes for shipping.

Eventually, Cinder finally walks over to my phone, puts one paw on it, and looks up at me questioningly.

"I'll just text him so he has my number," I decide, reaching for the phone. Which doesn't make a lot of sense, because honestly, we can still chat through the app. Still, exchanging numbers feels … different.

Marvin waves excitedly, the receipt with Rowan's number gripped tightly in one of his branches. He's been waiting—not patiently—all evening for me to relent.

"Give me that," I say.

He practically throws it at me.

"It's for the *investigation*," I tell him and Cinder.

If a mouse and a sentient mistletoe could sigh dramatically, then they would at that moment. Granny, floating in the corner and pretending very badly that she's not been eavesdropping all day, *does* give a dramatic sigh.

Then Marvin pelts me with a berry. *Hurry up*, he seems to say.

This is Ivy Winthrop, consultant on all things Fairhaven and disastrous.

. . .

A pause. The message has been delivered, but he doesn't answer. He's probably with Hartwood, I think, and grimace.

I put down the phone, feeling uncertain.

I get ready for bed. I apply a face mask. Moisturize. Oil my cuticles. Do a thousand other little self-care rituals that usually soothe me.

And check the phone a thousand times.

Eventually I get into my bed and pull up the quilted comforter. It was my grandmother's—she was a thread witch, like me.

But even that usually calming presence does not help me calm down. Why did I agree to help Rowan? Did I really think he could help with the ley lines? Or did I want to spend more time with him, to see if he was telling the truth about wanting to get to know me, outside of the investigation? Maybe there *is* something to Dahlia's palmistry app, after all.

Or not. What if he decides that I'm the reason the ley lines haven't healed? What if he tells the Concord? I'm already half-convinced that Hartwood is trying to find an excuse to kick me out of the Fairhaven coven; would the Concord kick me out of the United States witch registry altogether? For a witch not to have a coven is worse than being an orphan, I imagine. No registered witch is allowed to have contact with an unregistered witch—that means not Stella, not Ruby, not Marigold or Dahlia or even Rowan. I'd be completely cut off for the rest of my life.

With that reassuring thought running through my head, I—eventually—fall asleep.

CHAPTER 10

Just before 5:00 p.m., as I sit in my shop, sucking on my finger, which I've poked, *again*, with a needle—one might say I'm a little distracted—Rowan and Mabel show up with a wagon full of boxes.

"Busy this evening?" Rowan asks, giving me a charming smile.

I raise an eyebrow. He's wearing a black cotton shirt and jeans, with a well-worn black blazer, looking every inch the modern warlock—with a dash of dog hair.

"Why?" I ask, eyeing the boxes.

Mabel comes over and shoves her head under my hand for scratches. I oblige.

"Well, I've got approximately fifty volumes from my aunt's storage. I was thinking we could order some takeout and go through them together."

I narrow my eyes at him. Still, I can't deny that the fact that Rowan probably smuggled these books out from under Hartwood's nose—or even better, used his connection to the Concord to seize them from her—is kind of a turn-on. I wonder whose family grimoires are in those boxes, what memories and legacies might be returned to their owners. Still ...

"This is sounding suspiciously like a date, Rowan Hale," I say accusingly.

"Negative," he says, dragging the wagon up to my counter. "Strictly business. There are just a lot of books here, and I need an assistant if I want to finish this job and get back to Boston before next year. Besides, if I were asking you on a date, you'd know."

Something twinges in my chest. *Rowan ... leaving. Of course he's going to leave once this is over. All the more reason* not *to get involved.* Or so I try to tell myself.

"There's a pretty good Thai place a few blocks from here," I say, coming around the counter.

I open the first box—inside is an ancient grimoire, thick with dust. I wrinkle my nose. It smells like mildew. Clearly, Hartwood has not cared about storing these properly.

"My apartment is upstairs. Just let me lock the door, and we can take them up together," I say.

Rowan cocks his head to the side, a smile forming on his lips.

I roll my eyes. "I'm not … 'inviting you up,' Rowan," I say, my face heating. "It's … for the investigation. We'll need more space for this. Besides …" I flutter my lashes up at him. "If I were, you'd know."

"That's fair," he says, grabbing a few of the boxes. "At least let me buy you dinner. Consider it your consulting fee."

"Deal."

I lock up, grab a box, and head up the stairs, Cinder riding in my hoodie. I try not to think about the fact that Mr. Hale probably has an excellent view of my backside as we climb. I can only hope that the boxes he's carrying obscure it.

My heart is pounding for reasons beyond the handsome warlock being in my apartment. There's nothing in the kitchen or living room that's suspicious or would make him think I'm using unsanctioned magic. Unless he goes into my bedroom closet, or the craft room, he won't find anything incriminating. And there's certainly no reason for him to be in those rooms.

I open the door and am greeted by Marvin thumping down the hall, using his branches like arms to swing himself around like a leafy gorilla. Granny floats in from the living room, coming eye-to-eye with Rowan—though since she's so short, her feet only reach about his knees.

"And *who*, sir, might you be?" she asks, pointing a finger in his face.

"Granny, this is Rowan Hale, Hartwood's nephew. He's here to help us figure out the ley lines. Rowan, this is Granny. She's my great-something-grandmother."

"The pleasure is mine," Rowan says, giving her a smile.

I'm surprised to see Granny's pale, ghostly form turn slightly pink.

If he's at all surprised by seeing a ghost in my apartment, it doesn't show.

"Well, you just keep your hands off my granddaughter until you've proven yourself to be a warlock of good intentions. Do you hear me?" Granny says, her face stern.

Rowan nods. "I promise."

This seems to satisfy the old ghost, and she floats away, looking over her shoulder at Rowan again before disappearing through the wall.

"And this is …?" Rowan asks, looking at Marvin.

Marvin has climbed up onto one of the stools in my kitchen, cornered by a curious Mabel, whose tail is wagging a million times a minute. She keeps trying to sniff him, but Marvin shrinks back.

"This is Marvin. When Stella was a teenager, she thought it would be funny to enchant the Yule decorations. Ornaments floating around the house, that kind of thing. It wore off on everything except Marvin. He's been the unofficial town matchmaker ever since."

"And my aunt let you keep him?" Rowan asks. He puts down the boxes and gently restrains Mabel.

Marvin is shaking, his leaves rustling loudly. He throws a few berries at Mabel, who tries to snatch them out of the air like snacks. I'm not sure if they're poisonous to dogs, so I try to grab them before Mabel does. I *do* know that I accidentally swallowed one that Marvin tossed into a cup of my coffee once—and that evening my toilet and I became very well acquainted.

"There's no rule against keeping old enchantments, just making new ones," I say, and then I tell Marvin that if he keeps it up, I'm going to use him for next year's Beltane fire.

He droops, but at least he stops trying to poison Rowan's familiar.

"Anyway. That's why I kept the green hair. If I change it back, she'll know I'm using … that I've used magic. And no, hair dye doesn't work. I've tried."

Oops, I think. Nearly slipped there.

Rowan doesn't appear to notice. He simply adjusts his glasses and pats Mabel, who clearly wants to be Marvin's friend and *not* use him for a chew toy. She probably just wants to sniff him. Or maybe pee on him. I wouldn't stop her.

"Marvin, this is Mabel," I say, surprising myself with how gentle I sound, considering how much I hate the mistletoe. "She's very nice."

Marvin settles down and lets Mabel sniff him all over. Nobody gets peed on, and nobody gets poisoned. Satisfied, Mabel calms down and goes to sit at Rowan's side. Marvin, however, stays on the kitchen island, branches waving in the air.

"You said he's Stella's?" Rowan asks. He hefts one of the boxes onto the table. "Why is he here, then?"

I flush. "Um, he likes me."

Marvin pelts me with several berries.

"Also, he thinks I'm a lost cause when it comes to love, and if I don't say that, he'll keep throwing things at me." I've learned from past experience.

"I see," Rowan says, one side of his mouth twitching in a not-quite-there smile. "Well, let me order some food, and I'll show you what I've got so far."

"Have you ever considered … just leaving?" he asks, chewing on the last of the spring rolls.

We've put a healthy dent in the feast of Thai food that Rowan ordered, and my stomach is feeling full and happy. I was tempted to open a bottle of leftover wine from book club—*No, Ivy, that crosses into date territory*—but offered him lemonade instead.

"Of course I have," I say, handing him another box of books. "But Fairhaven is my *home*. My business is here. My friends. And I'm not giving up on it, not if there's a way to fix it."

Not to mention that recently I've felt … lost. I'm in my thirties. I have a job where I make decent money, but I have no friends other than Marigold, Stella, and Stella's family. I've never traveled, never gone to college beyond a few online courses that Hawthorne offers. I have no professional ambitions, just … no aim. No heading. Fixing up Fairhaven has given me purpose beyond just filling online orders, and now I'm determined that we're going to succeed.

At least we're making progress with the boxes, though most of what I've found so far has nothing to do with the ley lines. There is one article from what must have been an old witchy newspaper that I find interesting, and I show it to Rowan. It's yellowed and brittle with age, but the words are clear enough.

Ley Lines in the United States

Ley lines are invisible alignments of magical or energetic currents that criss-cross the earth, connecting sites of historical, spiritual, and mystical significance. In the United States, ley lines are a subject of both folkloric tradition and modern magical study, with various covens, geomancers, and independent researchers attempting to map and monitor their flow.

In recent years, the decline or instability of certain New England ley lines has raised concern among the magical community, prompting renewed interest in restoration techniques.

History

Interest in ley lines in America began in the early nineteenth century, when European settlers brought with them theories of "earth energies" from British folklore. This was further supplemented by the influx of Chinese immigrants, and their knowledge of "dragon paths," in the 1850s. By the late nineteenth century, occult societies, such as the Hermetic League of Alta California and the Salem Geomantic Circle, had published early maps suggesting that North America's ley network connected ancient indigenous sacred sites, colonial landmarks, and regions of natural magnetic anomalies.

Following the Great Flux Event of 1906, in which several ley currents reportedly shifted after the San Francisco earthquake, American witches began formalizing the study of ley energy under the emerging discipline of aetherometric geography.

Major Ley Convergences

Among the most well-documented ley intersections in the United States are:

- ***Mount Shasta, California**—long regarded as a site of powerful energy flow and spiritual manifestation*
- ***Salem, Massachusetts**—a historic convergence point where colonial witchcraft traditions overlap with older geomantic lines from Europe*
- ***Sedona, Arizona**—known for its towering rock formations and vortex phenomena, said to be surface manifestations of deep ley channels*
- ***Haleakalā Volcano, Hawaii**—the volcano is said to emit a frequency that matches the human heartbeat.*

*Additional ley lines of interest include **Coral Castle, Florida**—warlock and ley line historian Edward Leedskalnin built a castle there between 1923 and 1951. Of note is that this location sits at the crossroads of no less than nine ley lines, bested only by Stonehenge, at fourteen. **Boston, Massachusetts**, also boasts a convergence site, and the site of the American witch school, Hawthorne College. Nearby is **Fairhaven, Massachusetts**, a town once rich in magical resonance. According to local accounts, its ley lines have weakened in recent years, following a catastrophic magical event. Investigation is ongoing.*

Modern Research and Monitoring

The American Society of Ley Studies (ASLS), founded in 1945 after the Trinity nuclear test permanently altered ley lines in the American southwest, is the leading organization for documenting ley activity in the US. Using dowsing, geomagnetic analysis, and aetherometric instrumentation, ASLS researchers maintain a classified registry of active and dormant ley channels.

Rowan reads the article in moments and shakes his head.

Nothing helpful, then. I reach for the next box.

We're trying to find some historical documents, but all we've found is a lot of confiscated grimoires. I flip through them carefully. These should never have been removed from their families, much less stuffed unceremoniously into cardboard boxes. They are mostly in terrible condition, and it makes my heart ache to see them. A grimoire is a witch's—or warlock's—most important treasure. It can be passed down through a family for generations, chronicling history, spells, family lineages. Mine has become a book of experiments, though, of course, I don't admit to Rowan that mine is still *here*. Rowan seems equally affected—for a warlock whose magic is focused through words, spoken and written, to see these books kept in such a state … he looks positively stricken.

"I don't think we're going to have too much luck here," Rowan says, closing another book reverently. "I was hoping for something with the history of Fairhaven."

"We could try the library," I suggest. "No magical history, but you could learn more about the history of the town. Dahlia tried to put it all on the library website a few years back, but there's tons more in the actual building." It used to be one of my favorite haunts—mostly because I could check out as many romance and fantasy novels as I wanted. Also because no one would try to talk to me, to offer condolences or pithy religious quotes or anything. The librarians seemed to get this and had no problem aggressively hushing anyone who wanted to strike up a conversation with me.

Wonderful people, librarians.

"I read their website," Rowan says, nodding. He checks his watch.

It's getting late, though I don't have to open the shop tomorrow. I think of the online orders in my craft room, the ones I usually work on at night, with a pang in my chest. *It's okay, Ivy. You don't have to work* all *the time.*

"Can I ask you a question?" he says, taking a sip of his lemonade.

I twirl one last bite of pad thai around my fork. "Sure," I say, and pop it into my mouth.

"Can you tell me what happened that night? The accident?"

The pad thai suddenly feels like a glob of cement stuck in my throat. I manage to swallow it, and take a long drink while I collect my thoughts. I really should have seen this coming.

"Hasn't your aunt told you already?" I ask. My mind races, trying to decide how much to tell him, how much to trust him.

"I want to hear your side," Rowan says.

Mabel snores at his feet. Marvin stays on the kitchen island, though at least he's calm. Cinder, stuffed with edamame, has curled up in my hoodie, and I expect she is asleep as well. No one except me seems to feel the tension that's suddenly sprung up.

I swallow hard.

"It was about six months before I graduated high school," I say, haltingly. "Until then ... I wish you could have seen it. My dad would make pancakes for breakfast that flew around the kitchen like birds until you caught them. The dress I wore on the first day of senior year, I'd enchanted it so that the skirt became three inches shorter whenever my parents weren't looking. That was also around the time I changed my hair." I stop for a minute, lost in the memories. Goddess, they ache so, even all these years later.

Rowan, to his credit, doesn't push. He just waits for me to continue.

I take a deep breath.

"We used magic *all the time*. And it was beautiful," I say. "On Beltane, the fire would be a dozen times bigger. We would dance with glowing butterflies all night and invite our neighbors, the werewolves. We would have ten maypoles, and at least thirty witch kids running around, causing mayhem."

He looks a little astonished at this. "Other magical entities rarely contact us," he says slowly.

I shrug. "What can I say? We threw a hell of a party."

He smiles.

I take another sip of lemonade and continue. "And then I got sick." I hate remembering it—the sterile white walls of the hospitals, the needles, the periods of anxiety while waiting on results.

I think Rowan has stopped breathing. I meet his eyes for a minute and find myself steadied by their clear blue depths.

"Leukemia," I continue, looking away. "We treated it for a while. All my hair fell out." I twirl a strand of green hair around my fingers. I'll never forget what that felt like. The helplessness. The horror of watching my parents watch me fade away. "We tried all the usual spells too, of course, along with the chemo. Stella made me necklaces and bracelets out of quartz and bloodstone. I drank potions. We prayed under every full moon. We even went to the High Priestess of the Concord for advice. Nothing worked."

It was the darkest time of my life. Or so I'd thought.

"My parents … they researched endlessly. Then they found a spell in an Egyptian spellbook. It took them a while to prepare for it. It was the most complicated spell I've ever seen. One night they cast it together. I guess they hadn't prepared enough—there was a blackout that night. You can probably read about it in the old newspapers at the library. The ley lines surged, and I heard magic *shriek* as it was drained from the land.

"In the end, I woke up in the mayor's garden when the sun rose, completely healed. I've never had so much as a cold since. The doctors wanted to write an article about me, but Stella's mom sent them away and eventually, they left me alone.."

I stop, a lump in my throat stopping me from saying anything else.

"And … your parents?" Rowan asks gently. I shake my head, looking down at my calloused fingers and purple-lacquered nails, studying them instead of meeting his gaze.

"Since then, magic has been … unpredictable. Hartwood says my parents used too much, drained it too much. It needs to recover before we can use any more magic," I explain. "But I'm alive. And the ley lines are still a mess. And that is why your aunt hates me. And why most of the witches have left Fairhaven."

Rowan is quiet. Mabel senses something is off and lays her head in his lap.

Eventually I gather my courage and look up.

"I'm … so sorry," he says. His voice nearly cuts off as he speaks. "My aunt said they used a spell for their own gain. I never realized …"

"It was for me? Yeah," I say, smiling sadly. "They died, and all the magic in Fairhaven is gone. But I'm still here."

"You're still here," he echoes—but it sounds less like the sad end of a story and more like … maybe the beginning of one.

"Thank you for telling me, Ivy," he says. "You've given me a lot to think about."

"Well, if it helps get the magic back in Fairhaven, I'll tell you anything you want to know," I say, trying to be positive.

"Well … do you still have that spell? The one your parents used?" he asks cautiously.

I freeze. *Anything but that. Oh, and the stash of magic stuff in my closets.*

"Uh, it was destroyed with them," I blurt out. "Sorry."

"That's okay. There might be mention of it in the Concord archives somewhere," he says. "I've never heard of anything like it, though. If you can remember any of the particulars—the ingredients, the items, the moon cycle—anything could help. If this spell caused the problem, it might be the key to fixing it."

I've read that spell a thousand times. Memorized it backward and forward. There is nothing in that spell that would help. I know because I've tried.

"I think it was a new moon," I say. "That's all I remember. Sorry I can't be more help."

He nods, absently packing books up as he thinks. "That's all right. Thank you for everything," he says. "I think I'll try the library tomorrow. Would you … would you like to join me?"

I consider it for a moment. I *do* want to help him—I want magic back in Fairhaven for everyone. I just don't want to relive the worst day of my life over and over.

But tomorrow is Sunday, meaning I won't have to open the Golden Spindle. And Rowan has knowledge from the Concord, and access to the Concord archives. This *can't* be the only time something like this has happened. Rowan's right. We just have to keep looking.

"What time?" I ask.

CHAPTER 11

I pick my outfit the next morning with care.

"I want to look smart but not frumpy," I mutter to Cinder and Marvin—and mostly to myself—picking through my wardrobe. "What in here says 'sexy librarian'?"

In the end, I settle on a crisp white shirt and straight jeans, and pair them with a brown plaid blazer that definitely has that academic vibe. I smooth my hair back into a low bun, keep my makeup neutral, and pack up a small brown backpack with some notebooks and pens. The blazer has a pocket that I added in the front near my waist, where Cinder can ride unnoticed—because no women's blazers actually have functional pockets, and as a bespoke clothing designer, this is a hill I will die on. It *also* irks me to no end that most of the town will allow slobbery dogs—Mabel being the exception to the slobbering rule—everywhere, but they get all offended when I show up with a mouse. It doesn't help when I explain that Cinder is a very clean mouse, and that she bathes herself in my sink daily. Lavender bubble bath is her favorite.

It's a cool morning, with clear blue skies that promise to warm up the air by the afternoon. I meet Rowan in front of the Fairhaven Public Library. He looks annoyingly handsome in khakis and a cashmere cream-colored sweater. I can practically see myself curling up in it. The cuffs would be way over my hands, the hem probably halfway down my bare legs …

"Um, good morning," I say, hoping he thinks the flush in my cheeks is from the cold and not from me imagining peeling him out of that sweater. So I could steal it. Nothing more.

"Thanks for coming," he says, smiling, and my heart melts.

Be strong, Ivy.

"Yep," I reply, brilliantly.

Rowan ties Mabel to the bike rack and promises her we'll be back soon.

We head inside. The library is a beautiful old colonial-style building made of quaint red brick. It's one of the reasons I fell in love with my apartment—not only because it's directly above my shop, but for the industrial vibe and exposed brick in the same shades.

I show Rowan the front desk. Then we head for the historical section. There's a plaque commemorating the founding of the town in front of a shelf with all the local history books.

"1682," Rowan reads softly. The seal of the town is a sheaf of wheat crossed with an oak branch. Below, the town motto: *In equilibrio, sapientia.*

"I always thought it sounded a little witchy," I whisper.

We rifle through a few books but don't find anything more than a little snippet of town history—which I argue confirms my suspicions that the town was founded by witches.

Fairhaven was founded in 1682 by a company of families seeking safety and prosperity in the New World. This location was chosen for its fertile soil and balance of natural features, said to lend strength to the land and people.

Though they faced hardship in the early years, the settlement thrived. The community became known for its bountiful harvests, learned healers, and the uncommon health and longevity of its people.

Generations later, the town motto was born:

In balance, wisdom.

"Oh, this town was definitely founded by witches," Rowan whispers.

I nod.

That still doesn't help us, though. We need more about the ley lines.

We read on. But beyond those few vague mentions of a "balance of natural features" and "uncommon health and longevity," we find nothing more.

We take a break after a few unproductive hours to walk to Song's for coffee.

"Well, the wheat and oak branch on the town seal are crossed," I say, and sip my latte. "Just like two ley lines are crossed here."

"That's a stretch," Rowan says, frowning.

Song's Coffee Shop is full today, and we don't want to be overheard, so we decide to stroll down Main Street with our drinks instead.

"There's nothing else that you can think of?" Rowan asks.

"What about in the Concord's archives? Are they all digital? Have you checked?"

He sighs. "Even with the search function, there are dozens of volumes there, maybe more. It would take a team of us weeks to get through them all."

"Or ..." I stop myself.

He looks up. "Or what?"

"Um, or you could ask more people for help?"

"You're a terrible liar," he says, grinning. "Or what?"

I sigh. "Or you could cast a speed-reading spell. It would be easy for you. I used to do it all the time. Took me minutes to read a book for school."

He stops, eyebrows raised.

"I can't cast magic here," he says carefully. "My aunt has forbidden it. The ley lines are too unstable."

"So *she* says," I mutter.

He still hears me, though.

"Am I to risk the safety of the town just so I can read faster?" he asks.

I frown. I mean, the little magics I cast have never caused any major repercussions. Does he have to be so dramatic? Maybe he takes after Hartwood more than I thought.

"See? This is why I stopped myself from saying anything in the first place," I explain, walking faster.

Mabel cocks her head to the side, confused, but follows me.

"Where are you going?" Rowan asks, exasperated.

"I don't know!" I finish off my drink and toss the cup into a garbage can.

Rowan catches up to me, gently catching my hand in his. I could pull away if I wanted to.

I don't.

"We'll find the answers, Ivy. We just have to keep looking. It might take us longer this way, but we'll still get there."

We realize at the same time that he's still holding on to my hand—and he drops it, as if burned.

I sigh, hoping the movement will distract him from the heat flushing my face.

In her concealed pocket, Cinder wiggles, poking her nose out to check on me.

"Isn't there some way to, like, check on the health of the ley lines?" I ask.

He shakes his head. "There are some spells I could try, but they'd pull their strength from the ley lines and could endanger the town further."

"There's no, um, magical X-ray machine or lab test or something? An artifact, maybe?" I ask.

He shakes his head again.

Then stops.

"We could use an aetherometer," he says, lighting up. "I'd have to go back to Boston and get special permission—it's an antique, but there's one at Hawthorne's museum." He speaks to me, but mostly he's talking to himself, getting more and more excited. He rubs his hands together, thinking, a smile spreading on his face. "Yes, Ivy, that could work! It's probably how the original settlers here even found this place. They *must* have used one."

He's so excited that neither of us notices that he's thrown an arm around my waist to pull me in for a hug until it's too late.

We whirl, ending up face-to-face, and somehow his arms settle around me like they belong there. I take a startled breath in, and my chest meets his. Rowan's blue eyes are blown wide, dark centers so big they look like eclipses. He exhales slowly, the breath stirring the stray hairs on my forehead. Time is frozen around us, some crucial decision hanging in the balance—

And then he steps back, rubbing the back of his neck, which has turned crimson. I nearly stumble forward at the sudden lack of contact.

"Uh, sorry," Rowan says, taking another step back. "Got a little carried away. Um, I'm going to go make some calls and see if the, um, thing … the thing … the aetherometer … if I can get it."

Mabel comes over, fuzzy eyebrows furrowed, tail wagging, and ready to help if needed. He pats her head absently. My tongue must be fused to the roof of my mouth—I can't get a single word out. My skin is all tingly, and my heart is racing. I know this feeling, even if I won't admit it.

"Right," I manage to say finally. "Yes. Do that. I'll, um … I'm going to head home. It's getting late. And I have a lot of work to do."

It's barely midafternoon, but he doesn't correct me, just nods. I bet my face is as flushed as his is. Goddess, it's not like we're teenagers. I'm a grown woman with an apartment and a successful business and everything, damn it.

Though, apparently, my hormones still think I'm a teenager. Which is terribly unhelpful.

"Can I text you if I get the aetherometer?" he asks. "I could use a local to help me pinpoint the ley lines."

I nod. I'm fairly sure where the crossing of the ley lines is—or at least, where it was. I don't relish returning to that garden, but if it's the only way to help …

"Yes. I will," I say firmly.

Mabel gives a little *whuff* of encouragement, which shakes both of us out of our daze.

"I'll see you soon," Rowan says, smiling gently before walking away, getting lost in the crowd on the sidewalks.

Two days later I'm having brunch with Stella, Ruby, and Jacque outside our favorite casual restaurant, Maple & Main. Marigold supplies their breads, which is why their French toast is absolutely out of this world. Ruby and I always order it.

Today the sugar rush is only fueling her already rabid excitement over her upcoming birthday.

"And after the party with my friends, we're going to have the whole coven over! For me!" she says, eyes twinkling. "I can't wait to see what my familiar is going to be. I'm hoping for a unicorn or a red panda!"

Jacque laughs, shaking his head.

"I've never met a witch with a red panda familiar," Stella says with a laugh.

Ruby juts out her chin. "Yeah, there is one! A witch in Nepal! I saw it on the internet!"

"Unicorn! Unicorn!" Flossy shouts, wings flapping from her perch on the back of Stella's chair.

Stella rolls her eyes. "How about a raven, to keep Flossy company?"

Flossy eyes her suspiciously. "Unicorn!" she repeats, with more gusto this time.

Cinder sits neatly next to my plate, nibbling on a strawberry. Ruby eyes her thoughtfully, clearly imagining her own little animal friend.

"So, any more magic happening?" I ask. It's not uncommon for magic in teenage witches to start behaving … a little erratically. And not on purpose. Even Hartwood wouldn't fault Ruby for any errant magic.

"Your auntie Ivy here made all the roses in the mayor's garden bloom—in winter!" Stella says.

"I did," I say proudly, taking another huge bite of French toast.

"It would have been less conspicuous if the roses hadn't all been gold, no?" Jacque says.

Ruby starts laughing.

"Hartwood convinced the town it was a prank by the art college over in Haverhill," I tell Ruby.

She smiles, but it fades quickly. She looks down at her toast, making patterns in the maple syrup with her fork.

"She's worried because she hasn't had any magical … episodes yet," Stella whispers to me.

I nod. Well, she's got time before her birthday. Not everyone's "episodes" are as outlandish as mine were.

Though Stella did levitate Farmer Jackson's cow onto the barn roof once.

"Everyone comes into their magic in their own time," I say, patting Ruby's arm. "It's like … how some kids lose their teeth when they're five years old, and some not until later, right?"

"That's right!" Stella confirms.

"Are you hoping for healing magic, like your mom's?" I ask Ruby.

She shrugs, quiet and sullen.

"Sometimes it's word magic; sometimes it's healing, or something else," Stella says.

I nod. Well, whatever Ruby's familiar and magic end up being, I'm sure they'll suit her. Magic has a way of giving us exactly what we need, even if we don't know it at the time.

"More importantly, what are you going to *wear* for your party? And can I make it?" I ask.

Ruby perks up a little at this, and we scroll through ideas online for a few minutes. She gravitates toward red, and sparkly, and poofy. I can definitely work with that. Cinder lends a paw, pointing to things that catch her expert eye on my phone.

A shadow falls over us.

I look up, and it's Rowan, haloed by the sun, so bright I can hardly look at him.

"Oh," I say, shading my eyes. "Hello."

"Hello," he says, smiling at me. Holding my eyes longer than is necessary.

My heart rate has picked up at seeing him—probably because he startled me a little.

"Join us!" Stella says, grabbing a chair from the next little bistro table.

Rowan has no choice but to accept. Mabel sits next to Ruby, who gives her lots of pets—and a bit of sausage from her plate.

"Did you, um, find the thing … that you were looking for?" I ask awkwardly.

Rowan clears his throat, looking at the others at our table.

"It's okay. They know about the investigation," I say. I didn't see a reason to keep it secret.

"Oh. Yes, I found it. The aetherometer," he clarifies, for the others' benefit. "It's not really working at the moment, but I also got an old book with the original design and specifications, so I can probably figure it out."

"So you're a word warlock?" Ruby asks.

Rowan nods.

She asks him a number of rapid-fire questions about his magic, as if storing all the information away in case she ends up with word magic too.

"You should see my apartment back in Boston," Rowan confides. "It's completely covered in books. Shelves on all the walls, stacks of them everywhere. Even in my kitchen cabinets. There's no food, just books."

Ruby giggles.

Jacque looks offended that the kitchen might be considered storage space. To him, the space is nothing short of sacred. The only books allowed in the kitchen are cooking books that he himself has written, as Stella reminds us with a laugh.

A few minutes later, we pay our checks and get up to leave. Rowan takes my elbow gently and tugs me aside.

"Can I come by tonight?" he asks. My eyes must go as wide as our breakfast plates. "For the investigation," he says hurriedly. "I want to show you some of the books I found in Boston."

Stella and her family are already walking down the sidewalk toward their car—she turns and raises an eyebrow at me.

"Um, yes, all right," I say.

Rowan nods, and then he and Mabel head off in the opposite direction.

I run to catch up with Stella.

"What was that about?" Stella asks.

I flush. "He has some more questions for me. For the investigation," I explain, stumbling over the words.

Stella nods, one side of her mouth twitching up in a smile.

"He's *totally* into you," Ruby says.

Jacque snorts, then puts an arm around Ruby, pulling her close.

I roll my eyes, but I can't fight the warm feeling in my chest. *The feeling might be mutual.*

CHAPTER 12

Granny hovers over my shoulder in the kitchen as I stir a bubbling cauldron full of homemade spaghetti sauce, an old family recipe.

"*Two* of your great-aunts got their husbands with this recipe," Granny reminds me, before ordering me to add another pinch of salt. It's not like she can taste it, or smell it. She's just going off her gut and a few hundred years of experience, and that's never let me down yet.

And I just happen to know that Rowan likes Italian food.

No, I haven't eaten.

Good. Stop by Honey & Hearth on your way and pick up a baguette. I'm cooking pasta for us.

I catch myself smiling at my phone and put it down on the countertop. Tonight is *not* a date, I tell myself. I'm hungry. And I might as well feed the warlock who's going to help me save my town.

"More salt in the water, Ivy. Were you raised by werewolves?" Granny hollers.

I throw in another small spoonful of salt, and she nods in satisfaction. With fresh basil leaves from my windowsill and the homemade sauce, my apartment is smelling pretty fantastic. I'm not a great cook, by any means, but I've picked up a few things from Jacque and Granny along the way. Granny's always surprised me—for a woman who probably only ate gruel and unsalted bread her whole life, she's memorized several lifetimes of recipes from my various ancestors. She and Jacque have spirited conversations about them from time to time—pun intended.

A little while later, there's a knock on my door. I smooth my hair back and check my lipstick—*Why though, Ivy?*—and go open the door. Mabel rushes in, tail wagging so hard I nearly stumble when it hits me. She immediately goes to the stove, where Granny brandishes a ghostly ladle at her—*Where did* that *even come from?*

I can barely see Rowan behind the brown paper bags in his arms.

"Let me get that," I say, grabbing the top one, with one of Marigold's famous baguettes sticking out. It's heavier than I anticipated, and when I put it on the counter, I peek inside.

"Wine?" I ask, pulling out the bottle. It happens to be Potion Noir, an absolutely amazing pinot noir from a witch-owned winery in California.

"Um, I may have told Marigold I was coming over here and that you wanted bread. She wouldn't let me leave without this too," he says, flushing a little.

I sigh. "It's my favorite," I tell him, and he lights up.

"In that case, do you have a wine opener?" he asks, heading into the kitchen.

We nearly run into each other pulling the drawer next to the stove open, but eventually I get the wine opener and hand it to him.

Just as the pasta boils over like a volcano, water splashing and hissing as it contacts the stove.

"Oh, toadstools!" I cry, grabbing a towel and turning off the burner.

"You're *never* going to land a man if you can't make pasta proper-ly!" Granny scolds, positively scowling. There's boiling-hot water all over the stove and dripping onto the floor. Rowan has grabbed the paper towels by the sink and stoops to help me sop it all up. I stand, intending to take them from him, just as he bends down—

And the top of my head smashes right into his nose.

"You know, in Boston I'd have already cast a healing spell on this," Rowan says, a bag of frozen peas held to his nose.

I'm just grateful that I didn't break his glasses.

"And I'd have cast a cleaning spell on *this*," I say, gesturing at my kitchen disaster.

Satisfied that he's only bruised, not broken, I go back to the kitchen and grab two wineglasses. One of them has little moon phases etched on it; the other I got from a yard sale. It's painted in ombré blue, and it's one of my favorites. I pour us both a generous amount and set the moon glass in front of Rowan. I busy myself making big bowls of spaghetti, too embarrassed to try to make conversation. Granny fled the scene ages ago, once it was obvious that I'd completely botched any possible romance. Not even her spaghetti sauce recipe can save me now.

"Really, I'm fine," Rowan says.

I narrow my eyes at him and plop a giant bowl of spaghetti in front of him.

"Thank the goddess this *wasn't* a date," I say, twirling some spaghetti around my fork. I take a bite with relish—Granny's recipe really *is* that good, even if it did take me hours to make. "You'd never want to see me again."

"Not a date. I didn't bring flowers, remember?" he says, his smile made a little more goofy by the bag of defrosting vegetables on his nose.

"Are you *sure* it's not broken?" I ask for the fifteenth time, biting my lip.

"Pretty sure," he says, gingerly touching his nose. It's slightly swollen but not bruised or bleeding. I don't know a lot about healing, but I think that's a good sign.

"Maybe we should see if Stella can come over and take a look," I say—also for the fifteenth time.

"I'm fine," Rowan says, again. "Your concern is … touching."

"I just don't need Hartwood casting me out of the coven for maiming her nephew," I tell him.

He considers this.

"On that note," he says, taking a long drink of his wine. "Hey. This is really good."

"Told you," I say smugly, enjoying my own glass.

"Yes. So I have the aetherometer here. I was planning to spend some time on the diagram specifications tonight," he says, motioning to the case at his side. "But this spaghetti is a much better idea."

"Granny's recipe," I say. "I remembered what you said about keeping books in your kitchen cabinets earlier. Thought it might be nice to have a home-cooked meal. I don't imagine Hartwood is the domestic, cooker-of-family-meals type."

He holds my eyes for a moment, like he's trying to puzzle me out.

"Yes," he repeats simply. "Thank you."

"You're welcome," I say.

The awkward silence stretches between us like saltwater taffy.

Broken, fortunately, by Mabel stealing a piece of Marigold's baguette off my plate.

"Can I ask why you named her Mabel?" I ask, munching on my own bread.

He nearly sputters on his wine. "Um, I meant to name her Maple. Because she's the color of maple syrup. My family misheard me," he says sheepishly. He ruffles the dog's ears, and her tongue lolls as she smiles in the way only a golden retriever can. "But I think Mabel suits her."

"It does. She's a classy lady," I say.

"And Cinder?" he asks, gesturing toward my mouse, who is nearly passed out in contentment with a very full belly.

Cinder cracks an eye open at her name, then sighs and snuggles back into the nest she's made of my napkin.

"I always liked to make my own clothes. I took a pair of heels once and bedazzled them all over, because I wanted real glass slippers. The kids at school used to call me Cinderella," I say with an expression that is part smile and part grimace. "I was surprised by Cinder." I stroke her soft gray fur. "But she's the best helper you can imagine, and she's got great taste."

"There aren't many witch children left in Fairhaven, are there?" he asks, twirling another bite of spaghetti.

"Ruby's the next to have her claiming day. Then River, Dahlia's little brother," I explain. "After that it will be a while for Peony. Some —well, a lot of witches left after the accident, and the rest after Madam Hartwood's proclamation." I pour us both another glass of wine.

He helps me clear the table and clean up without being asked— again, I'm glad it's not a date, because he'd be miles beyond any other man I've had over. Goddess, my standards feel so low they might as well be a limbo stick.

Then we tackle the aetherometer. It looks like a baroque clock. Rowan says it was modeled on a ship's chronometer, balanced so no matter what the waves—or magic—threw at it, it would remain accurate. The wood is old and dark and chipped, the glass of the cover scratched with age.

"How old *is* it?" I ask.

"Over three hundred years," he says. "I had to practically promise the curator a kidney before he'd let me take it."

He opens the glass front panel. There's a circular meter inside, but instead of twelve numbers, like on a clock, it goes from one to one hundred.

"That's the relative power gauge," he says.

At the bottom, there's a small drawer. He opens it. Inside is a small glass canister, dark and smudged with age, with coppery fittings on either end. It slots into the drawer like a battery.

Inside the glass is something that looks like mercury, silvery and shining and fluid, but suspended as if in a gaseous form.

"Aether," Rowan says, almost reverently.

"Hence, aetherometer," I whisper. I'm not sure why we're whispering. Maybe it's being so close to a part of our own history, close to something so rare.

And without me realizing it, so close to each other. In an effort to get close to the aether, to actual condensed magic, I'm leaning right up against Rowan. And definitely not noticing how he smells like soap and piney aftershave.

"It's gorgeous," I say.

Rowan clears his throat, looking back at the aether. "Yes. Yes, it is."

CHAPTER 13

The Hunter's Moon is due on the day of the Fairhaven Halloween festival. Marigold traditionally makes the bulk of the day's goodies—pumpkin pies to be won on the cakewalk, pumpkin cupcakes to be devoured by everyone, and six kinds of pumpkin bread. Song has got the booth next to her on Main Street, conveniently outside her shop, and across the street from my apartment, so a pumpkin spice latte is the first order of business for me today. She's also serving warm apple cider and regular black coffee. I'm savoring my first sip of latte, the sweetness and caffeine as good as real magic in my veins, when I hear my name being called.

Rowan and Mabel are walking over to me. Rowan's arms are full with two bales of straw. I grin as he approaches, and pluck a few stray straws from his shirt and hair.

"I'm helping out with the straw bales," he says.

"I see that," I say through my grin.

He laughs. "Yeah, I guess you do. I should be done soon, though. What's the best part of this festival? It's my first one, and I don't want to miss out."

I fill him in as I wave to Marigold and her bakery assistant, Moth. Today Timothy "Moth" Jenkins is decked out in their finest drag, showcasing their alter ego, Brooma Thurman, a caricature witch. They are wearing a wig inspired by *Pulp Fiction*, with high heels, fish nets, a short black dress, and a lofty pointed black hat.

Moth is one of the few humans who know who we really are—the witches, I mean. Marigold has been working with them for years, and they've earned her trust—and therefore mine and Stella's. Brooma Thurman has become a beloved figure at the library for Children's Book Hour, and sometimes dresses up at work too. Today Marigold is wearing a black dress and pointy hat as well, though substantially less flamboyant. Moth is calling out the list of all the goodies they have for us today, and they're already drawing a crowd.

"And Farmer Brown usually sets up an apple cannon at the end of the street with bushels of rotten apples for the kids to shoot at targets —the winner last year got a baby goat." I grin, remembering Iris's horror when River came up to her, baby goat in his arms and a giant smile on his face. She relented eventually, and Socks the goat—so called because he liked to eat socks, not because he had any white markings—became a beloved member of their family. Though I think Iris secretly wishes she could curse Farmer Brown.

"Apple cannon? That sounds … fun," Rowan says, eyebrows high.

"Wait until you see the Punkin Chunker," I say with a wicked grin.

"No," he says. "Farmer Brown again?"

"Yep," I say. "His goal is to break a mile. The man loves two things: farming and shooting his produce from cannons."

"This I'll have to see," Rowan says. "Will you let me know when the … pumpkin chucking starts?"

"Punkin chunkin'," I correct him. "And trust me, you'll hear it."

He grins. "I'd like to go see it with you anyway, if that's all right with you."

I flush and take another sip of my latte. My knitted hat and scarf feel suddenly too warm.

"Um, sure," I say. "Just … come find me when you're done with the straw."

Cinder climbs up my shoulder and makes herself comfortable on my scarf there.

"Okay," he says. "See you soon."

He and Mabel walk off. I definitely do not watch.

"Hey!" Stella says, surprising me from behind with a giant hug. Thank the goddess my coffee has a lid.

"Hey, yourself!" I say, hugging her back.

She's wearing all black with an ironic witch's hat—I love that most of the coven dresses up like actual witches today, and we just blend in with the costumes. It would be nice to be known and accepted in our town, but the humans just aren't ready for that kind of thing. Countless towns all over the world have had their supernatural residents try to integrate over thousands of years of history, and inevitably it ends in bloodshed.

But today? Today we proudly wear our witchy wardrobes, and the town has no idea.

My knitted hat is a black witch hat. I'm wearing a full tulle skirt that swishes when I walk, and black pointy boots. And I love it.

"Where are Ruby and Jacque?" I ask, looking behind her.

Stella frowns. "Ruby's sick."

I sob dramatically for a moment. For Ruby to miss the Halloween festival, and then our Samhain? She's got to be *really* sick, and probably really heartbroken.

"Is she okay?" I ask.

"I think so," Stella says. "Just a fever. No appetite. Wants to sleep all day. I've given her some meds, and Jacque's keeping an eye on her. I just wish ..."

Her wish goes unsaid, but we both know what she's thinking. *I wish I could cast a healing spell and relieve her suffering.*

"It's probably just a cold," I say, looping my arm through Stella's. "There's lots of that going around this time of year."

"Yeah," Stella says, more morose than I've seen her in ages. "I just hope she's feeling better for her claiming."

"That's ages away," I say reassuringly. "I'm sure she'll be back to herself in a few days."

"Back to herself!" Flossy agrees, landing on Stella's shoulder.

Stella strokes the parrot's feathers. "Right," she says, then straightens. "Come on. I promised Ruby I'd win her a prize today."

"A baby goat?" I ask.

In the distance, I hear the boom of the apple cannon and the squealing of excited children.

"Um, no," Stella says, laughing. "I was thinking a caramel apple and maybe a stuffed animal."

"A caramel apple? Says the *dentist*?" I ask, one hand on my heart in astonishment.

Stella shrugs. "She loves them. We'll make sure to floss after."

"Floss after!" Flossy agrees. Flossy then spots Marigold and Biscuit, and she takes off to receive the snacks that Marigold invariably has for her. Moth *loves* Flossy, who absolutely preens under their attention.

Main Street has been shut down to cars for the day. Strings of paper lanterns crisscross the street. Straw bales are stacked strategically by scarecrows and piles of pumpkins for decoration and photo ops. There's the weighing area for the county's largest pumpkin, a booth where if a player knocks over all the bottles, they get to hit the school principal in the face with a pie, and a stainless-steel tub filled with water and apples for bobbing.

"I usually have to fix a few loose teeth after that one," Stella confides, nodding at the tank. Some overzealous teenagers are bound to knock their heads together.

We wave to Marigold and Moth, who are working hard, as usual, between the stacks of baked goods and homemade honey, and head to the caramel apple booth. I buy a giant bag of kettle corn; Stella gets two caramel apples.

"One for Jacque," she confides. "He's a food snob, but he loves these."

"So that's where Ruby gets it from," I tease.

Stella shrugs.

It actually doesn't take us all that long to get down Main Street— the crowd each year is getting smaller and smaller, and there are fewer vendors. When I was little, this festival would draw tourists from all over. Now, even though everyone is doing their best to bring the holiday cheer, it feels … lonely. There are maybe a dozen kids in costumes running around—dressed as superheroes and cats and ninjas. The local vendors aren't selling much; Stella and I buy a few more things in the interest of supporting them. I don't really *need* a pair of pumpkin candles, or pumpkin spice bubble bath—okay, I have a pumpkin spice problem—but I happily add them to my purchases. A solitary fiddle player tries to lighten up the scene with lively music; a few crumpled bills sit in his open case.

Eventually Rowan and Mabel catch up to us. Mabel has an orange handkerchief tied around her neck. Rowan is wearing khakis and a black sweater with the sleeves pushed up, a few stray strands of straw still sticking to him.

A large *BOOM* echoes down Main Street, and the small crowd surges toward the end like it's the starting gun they've all been waiting for. Rowan jumps, his glasses tilting slightly on his nose. He pushes them back up and looks at me with a question on his face.

"Come on," I say, grinning. I grab his hand and pull him down the street. "That's the punkin chunker."

At dusk, the town meets back on Main Street, and we begin the tradition of carrying lighted lanterns to the mayor's garden. It's more of a park than a garden, really, with neat beds of flowers and little stone paths and embellished metal benches. The story goes that the town was founded right here, and that the mayor's house was the first to be built. Locals attribute the beautiful garden to the masterful local gardeners and rich soil.

We witches know better. The garden is precisely at the crossing of the ley lines, and that is exactly where Rowan and I will be checking with the aetherometer later tonight. I've always loved the subtle way our town blends the supernatural and tradition. It honestly lets us get away with so much.

As night falls, the humans begin to disperse, leaving their lighted lanterns in the garden. It lights it up beautifully, though the flowers aren't as abundant as they once were. In the center is a small metal firepit—a far cry from the bonfire we used to set for Beltane, but Hartwood claims it is symbolic. She looks the part of a real witch tonight, in her plain black dress and pointed hat, more so than I do in my costumy look, or Stella in her sleek, modern take on our traditional outfits. We have quiet conversations about the festival and whether Farmer Brown will break his record distance next year, and whether Brooma Thurman's costume this year was better than last year's—it was, definitely.

"We used to write our wishes for the year on scraps of paper and toss them in," I tell Rowan. Standing next to the fire with him, surrounded by lantern light, my stomach full of sweets and my blood singing with caffeine, I wish I could somehow bottle this feeling, to save it and keep it with me forever.

"Now we're not even allowed to do that," Stella whispers.

Hartwood's flinty eyes cut to us, her thin mouth downturned, as usual. She might not like us, but she can't keep us from participating in coven events.

It's a solemn ceremony, when we *should* be celebrating the harvest and the bounty the goddess has given us this year with songs and laughter. I make a silent vow to myself that when Rowan and I return magic to Fairhaven, we're going to revive these ceremonies, not mourn during them.

I square my shoulders and wait for Hartwood's long-winded speech to finish.

The rest of the coven departs soon after. Marigold, looking exhausted, carries a snoozing Biscuit out of the garden, barely noticing where she's going.

"I need to check on Ruby," Stella says, reaching into a pocket for her phone.

"Go on," I tell her.

Her eyes are already fixed on the screen, fingers quickly typing away.

Hartwood shoots a look at me, where I stand by the fire with Rowan. That look probably could have frozen the fire solid. Even Salem is glaring at us.

But not even the coven's mother is allowed to cast magic. All she can do is cast dirty glances and snide comments when she knows I'm in earshot.

Not that it matters to me.

Eventually Hartwood and her elderly friends leave the garden. It's near midnight, the full moon sailing high overhead. Rowan takes the aetherometer from its case, which looks like an old leather suitcase. He plays with the dials a moment before closing the glass door on the front. He sets it near the fire, theoretically where the crossing of the ley lines is the strongest—where the original witches founded the town.

"Now what?" I ask. The aetherometer is just ... sitting there.

"It's supposed to take a few minutes to get the readings," Rowan says, pushing his glasses back up on his nose. "Hopefully, we'll see the dials start ticking upward soon. At Salem, the readings are close to ninety-five most of the time. That's some of the highest in America. It was probably eighty or ninety here at one point. From what my aunt says, I expect we'll see closer to twenty or twenty-five. At those levels, even minor magics can be disruptive."

I crouch to look at the aetherometer. Inside, the aether is starting to wake up. It glows a little, shining light blue, and whirls like thick fog.

Rowan bends down beside me, and I swear we're both holding our breath as we wait for the gauge to move.

The needle twitches. Then twitches again, like a heart beating.

The needle moves up to five and then settles back down. I let out a low whistle.

"Five? Is that all we're getting?" I ask, disappointment curdling in my gut. The ley lines are worse off than I thought. Guilt floods me— have I done that? My little spells? Have I made it worse when all I want to do is make it better?

Before Rowan can answer me, the gauge goes wild, spinning around and lapping past the one hundred mark once, twice, more times than I can keep track of. Rowan inhales sharply, his eyes wide.

And then the whole thing explodes.

CHAPTER 14

Rowan is bleeding pretty badly, probably because the idiot threw himself over me when the aetherometer exploded, and now we're both in shock. As I wrap my scarf around his bloody arm, he grabs what is left of the aetherometer and stuffs it into its case, and then we limp toward my apartment as fast as we can go.

There was some shouting after the explosion, and I'm sure I heard someone yell "Bomb in the mayor's garden!" hysterically when we left. I can just hear the first sirens when we reach my apartment door. We smell like sulfur and smoke. Mabel is so frantic she's whining and twining around our legs so much I can barely walk, while Cinder has decided that my hair is the safest place to be—my hat was knocked off during the blast; no idea what happened to it—and I can feel her tight little paws pulling at the strands as I move.

"Gauze, gauze, where are you?" I mutter, combing through the junk drawer in my kitchen for something clean to wrap around Rowan's arm.

Marvin is trying to help, his branchy arms opening and shutting drawers for all they are worth. Granny is nowhere to be found.

"Do you have healing incense?" Rowan asks.

I freeze. "Of course I do," I tell him. I'm a proper witch, even if I haven't been able to practice like one.

"Can I have it? And a white candle?"

He's asking for a healing spell.

"We're not allowed to do magic," I remind him.

"I think it's safe to say that the *lack* of magic is not the problem in this town," he says wryly. Blood is starting to seep through the scarf wrapped around his arm, the red stain slowly spreading.

"Oh, toadstools," I say, and I run from the room.

I pull out the box of magical items from under my bed and start sorting through them. I immediately find the incense, a mixture of juniper and rosemary.

The candles, though, are nowhere to be found.

I go back to the kitchen and light the incense. I haven't smelled incense in ages, and for a moment, I almost forget the warlock *bleeding out on my kitchen table.* Almost. I inhale, the fumes steadying me, and have an idea.

I grab my bag of goodies from the festival and pull out one of the pumpkin-scented candles.

Which is, conveniently, white.

Rowan raises an eyebrow, and the side of his mouth quirks, but he doesn't comment. He's checking Mabel over for injuries—thankfully, she has none, though she's still whining and laying her head on his lap. I light the candle and set both it and the incense in front of him. His lips are already moving, muttering a spell to the goddess for healing.

> *By rain and flame, by breath and stone,*
> *Let pain be eased, let strength be grown.*
> *Light within, restore, renew,*
> *Blood and body, healing true.*

The candle flickers, and I catch my breath. It's such a surreal moment —and one that might just change the fate of my town.

Maybe even my life.

Rowan peels back the saturated scarf from his arm. There's a gash clean through his sweater where the shard of glass struck him—but the skin beneath it is intact. I use the end of the scarf to wipe the blood from his skin—he's healed. Whole.

I look up at him, relieved—and he's staring down at me. He cups my face with his other hand, and I feel his thumb rub over a sore spot.

"You're hurt too," he says, though it comes out more like a whisper.

Now that the adrenaline is wearing off a little, now that I'm sure Rowan isn't going to bleed to death and I don't need to rush him to the emergency room, I can feel a dozen small cuts, like splinters, on my face and hands. The glass front of the aetherometer must have shattered and cut us both.

Rowan repeats his spell, and the pains in my face fade away. His hand, though, lingers on my cheek for a moment.

"Rowan," I ask, and swallow hard. "What does this mean?" My gaze tears away from his, finally, and moves toward the leather suitcase by the door.

Cinder scurries down from my hair and assesses my face from the kitchen table. Then she unleashes a barrage of angry squeaks that I can only assume mean she is *pissed* at the risk I took tonight.

"I know. I'm sorry. I don't know what happened," I say, trying to appease her.

She bites the air, baring her teeth at me, then scurries away to pout.

"She'll be fine," I tell Rowan. "She's just a little dramatic sometimes."

"I … I don't know what it means," Rowan says, and he runs a hand through his curls, making them stand on end. "I'm going to call one of the professors back at the college. Maybe he'll know."

"I'm going to take a shower." I look at the singes and ash and blood on my dress and sigh. "Can I get you a drink or something first?"

"A drink would be great," he says, and as he fishes around for his phone, I pour us both a large glass of Potion Noir. It is my favorite, after all.

I hear Rowan apologizing for the late hour to someone on the phone while I head to the bathroom—it's nearly 1:00 a.m., and I'm completely exhausted. I take a quick, warm shower, rinsing the dried blood and smell of smoke from my hair, and towel off.

By the time I'm done getting dressed in a pair of comfy sweatpants and a *Fairhaven* T-shirt, I don't hear Rowan on the phone anymore. I towel-dry my hair as I walk into the living room—he's sitting in my big chair, wineglass at his side almost untouched. Mabel has a blanket in her mouth and is drawing it up and over him—and he's sound asleep, his glasses skewed to one side. Mabel looks at me pointedly, as if telling me *not* to wake up her warlock under any circumstances. Marvin is sitting on the kitchen table, surprisingly quiet and still, like he's sleeping, or trying to puzzle out what in the goddess's name just happened.

I douse the lights. I remove Rowan's glasses and set them by his wineglass. I don't really want to leave him sleeping alone, for some reason, so I grab my quilt from my bedroom and haul it to the small loveseat in the living room. From there, I can keep an eye on Rowan, and hopefully, I'll wake up if he does. I need to know what he found out on his phone call, and what that means for Fairhaven.

Cinder crawls up the loveseat and curls up on the throw pillow I'm lying on. She squeaks once, in apology, and licks my face. I pet her silky fur, reassuring her that I'm all right, and drift off to sleep in moments.

When I wake in the morning, I'm momentarily confused. I'm sleeping on my couch, which I never do.

I bolt upright, smoothing my hair back from my face—goddess, I fell asleep with wet hair; I bet it looks amazing right now—and look for Rowan. His blanket is folded neatly on my chair, but he's nowhere to be seen. I pad to the kitchen—the aetherometer case is still there.

Cinder runs up my leg and plops into my pants pocket. She wiggles for a minute to get comfortable.

The door unlocks with a click.

And in comes Rowan and Mabel, with an armful of brown paper bags.

"Um, good morning," Rowan says, a sheepish blush on his face—or maybe that's just the cool autumn air blowing in with him. "Mabel needed a walk. And I needed coffee. I thought you might be hungry."

My stomach growls in agreement, especially when the smell of Marigold's pumpkin spice cinnamon buns hits my nose. I grab plates, and Rowan sets out the buns and lattes from Song's for both of us. I frantically pull my hair back into a messy bun and run my hands over my face—goddess, I hope I remembered to wash my eyeliner off last night.

"Are we, um, going to talk about what happened last night?"

Rowan freezes, his pale face going even paler. "Yeah, I'm sorry for passing out like that, and staying the night. Actually, casting magic has always taken a lot out of me. I think that's why I gravitate toward books and words more."

I shake my head. "I meant the aetherometer exploding."

"Oh, yeah," he says, rubbing the back of his neck.

I grin a little at his discomfort and dig in to my breakfast. It's *amazing*.

"So I talked to my professor back at Hawthorne College, Dr. Hallowell. He's the one I borrowed the aetherometer from. He curates the college's museum," Rowan explains, digging in to his own cinnamon bun. He savors it with a look of pure bliss. "Goddess, Marigold's baking is incredible," he says. "Anyway, Thad—Dr. Hallowell—was mostly just mad at me for destroying the aetherometer. He didn't believe me at first, thought I was trying to cover up dropping it or something. But when I explained what had happened with the rainbow the other day, and the green fire, he started to believe me. He thinks there's something *wrong* with the ley lines— they're clearly not fading, no matter what my aunt says. If anything, they're *over*powered. We just have to find out how, and why, so we can fix them."

"Has he heard of anything like this happening before?" I ask, sipping my latte.

Cinder scurries out of my pocket to steal a piece of my bun.

"No," Rowan says, shaking his head. "He's going to do some research and get back to me. Someone at the college must have an idea of what's going on."

Not for the first time, I feel the weight of my own ignorance. I never applied to Hawthorne College after high school—I took some online classes in magical fashion design, but that was it. Higher-level witch learning? It's not for me. Neither of my parents went, though most of the older witch families, like Rowan's, all go.

Still, to be in a place with other witches? Where I wouldn't have to hide who I was? Where magic is embraced and practiced and perfected? I wonder if it's too late for me to consider it.

"So, what's the next step here?" I ask.

Rowan sighs. "The last spell cast before the ley lines started misbehaving was the healing spell your parents cast. You said it was Egyptian—you really don't remember anything else about it?"

I bristle. "I told you I didn't."

He runs a hand through his curls. "I know. I just hoped maybe you'd remembered something. That spell could be the key to unraveling this."

My gut clenches. Maybe it would be, maybe not. All I know is that was the worst night of my life, and I have no desire to relive it.

Just then, Granny decides to materialize halfway through my kitchen wall.

"Have you checked those books in your crafting room?" she asks.

I freeze.

"What books?" Rowan asks, his interest as a word warlock clearly piqued.

"I ... well, promise you won't tell your aunt," I say, pointing my finger at him.

Rowan laughs. "Which part? Exploding a priceless museum artifact? Sleeping over at your apartment?"

"I meant the book ... and you didn't *sleep over* sleep over," I say, my face heating. "You just ... spent the night."

Rowan raises an eyebrow.

"You spent the night?" Granny cackles. Then she glares at me. "Hussy."

"Granny!" I shout, mortified.

"I promise not to tell my aunt anything that transpires between the two of us. Will that do?" Rowan asks.

I know he's playing with those words, but I nod, face positively radioactive. The last thing I need is Hartwood thinking there's something between us. Otherwise, when magic is back—well, I guess it never really left—I'll be the first one she'll hex. And it'll be something devious, too. Like every time I drink coffee, it will burn my tongue.

Actually, I'm going to remember that one, just in case.

I take Rowan to my crafting room, which for some reason feels oddly intimate.

"Look, I've … been doing magic this whole time," I confess in a rush.

Rowan waits for me to continue, one eyebrow raised.

"And I kept my family grimoires. I told Hartwood that they must have hidden them, but that's a lie. I have them."

I open the door to my workroom. Granny materializes through the wall that the room shares with the kitchen.

Rowan looks around with an unreadable expression. He takes in the piles of boxes for the orb purses I've recently finished, the neatly stacked bolts of fabric, the yarn, the sewing machine, and the rest of the mundane things.

He also notes a gauzy dress on the mannequin in the corner, drifting in a wind that isn't there. And the twinkling sequins on a skirt, which sparkle in lights that aren't there. He takes in the embroidery on a scarf, which is stitching itself into curling vines and flowers.

"I knew you were a thread witch, but this room … I can feel how special it is," Rowan says.

My heart warms. Part of me was worried he'd hate it—Rowan, the academic, the college-educated. That he'd look down on it, or find it … basic, for lack of a better term.

"Thank you," I say, and mean it.

"Now show him the books," Granny chimes in. "He's got word magic. He wants to see the words!"

I take a deep breath and open the door to the room's closet. I open the top box and take out the first book—my grimoire.

"This one's mine," I tell him, and set it on my worktable. "I started it after the accident, so there's nothing relevant in there for you."

Reading another witch's grimoire is akin to reading their diary, and it is kept just as secret. Rowan acknowledges my request with a nod.

I pull out a box of books, which is heavy and coated with dust. Rowan takes it and sets it on my worktable reverently.

"May I?" he asks.

I nod, unable to speak. I blame the dust clogging my throat. *I have to let him in*, I tell myself. *I have to trust that he knows what he's doing. That this will fix Fairhaven.*

Rowan doesn't rush. He takes each book out, inspects its binding as if he's looking for a curse or hex for when the wrong person opens it. When he finds my mother's grimoire, he pauses, looking to me for permission. I nod again.

He spends a long time reading it. Eventually I step out and make us some tea and snacks. Cinder busies herself with some complicated embroidery on the gauzy dress—she's a wonder with a needle and thread—while Mabel contentedly sleeps at Rowan's feet, her head propped on his shoes. It's a cozy, contented scene—but my heart is hammering against my ribs the entire time.

Eventually he comes to it. I know the second he does. His gaze shoots to mine, eyes wide.

"I thought maybe she referenced the Ebers Papyrus, or the London Medical Papyrus," he whispers. "This is …"

"Divine intervention," I finish.

CHAPTER 15

We take my mother's grimoire to the kitchen. It's past noon, and honestly, I need something in my stomach besides sugar and caffeine if I'm going to dive into my mother's innermost thoughts.

"Have you read this?" Rowan asks, gently turning another page. He's seated at the table, and so invested in reading he barely notices when I place a sandwich beside him—he takes a bite and chews absently.

"I have. Once. A long time ago," I say. "I've read the last spell a few hundred times. I haven't been able to come up with anything."

He wordlessly turns another page, finds it empty, and turns back.

"This is an oracular amuletic decree," he says, eyes still on the book. "I didn't think anyone had written one in three thousand years."

"My parents were desperate," I tell him. "I believe my father had a contact in Egypt that may have helped, but I've never been able to find out who."

"This sounds like a prayer to Nekhbet … Are you all right if I take a photo? I'd like to send it to Thad and see what he thinks."

My chest squeezes.

"All right," I manage to wheeze.

He snaps the photo with his phone, and a photo of the spell that killed my parents zooms away to a museum curator in Boston. Marvin helpfully plates some cheese and crackers for me to eat. The plant might have matchmaking in his veins—I guess plants do have veins in a certain sense—but he *is* a damn decent roommate when he isn't pelting me with mildly poisonous berries.

Rowan begins to read aloud, his voice soft and low. I'm not even sure he knows what he's doing, but I can feel panic settling into my brain, the rational side fleeing as scenes from the accident flash before me. My heart rate spikes, and a cold sweat breaks out on my neck.

> *I shall keep her healthy in her flesh and her bones.*
> *I shall protect her and I shall look after her.*
> *I shall be between her and any sickness.*
> *I shall grant her life, health, and a great and goodly old age.*

I say the last line with him, having memorized it years ago. His gaze flickers to mine again, and that's all it takes to put me into full fight-or-flight mode.

I choose flight.

I flee to my bedroom, slamming the door and locking it. Cinder squeezes through the gap between the carpet and the door, squeaking with alarm.

I head to the bathroom and turn on the shower, hoping the water will drown out the sound of my sobs, which are coming in great, gasping breaths.

I slump to the floor, my hands and feet as cold as ice, my fingers trembling like leaves in the wind. Flashes of *that night* run through my head. My parents, chanting the prayer with their arms raised to the sky. The sky dark, the stars obscured by thick thunderclouds. Sitting on the wet grass between them, cold and sick and shaking one minute —and warm and healed the next. I looked down at my hands then, as I do now.

But then a lightning strike—natural, or a result of the immense magic they wielded—took both of my parents from me in a single instant.

The door crashes open, and I can't help it—I scream, scrabbling back against the bathtub.

Rowan stands there. Just Rowan. No lightning. He looks alarmed, but unharmed.

"Um, I used an unlocking spell," he says, gesturing at the door-knob. "Sorry. I just wanted to check … are you okay?"

He crouches down beside me and smooths a strand of hair back from my face. It's stuck to my skin with tears. I wipe the arm of my sweater across my face in an effort to clear it, but I see the thick smudge of mascara on the sleeve that indicates I probably just made it all worse.

Rowan sits beside me, folding his long legs up, and just gently leans his shoulder against mine. Mabel sits at the door, whining and pawing at the floor, but unsure if she should approach. I half laugh, half sob, and throw my arms open to her—she flies into us both, her long tongue licking my face all over, throwing her full warm, comforting weight against me. Cinder squeaks and retreats to my hair but doesn't throw her usual tantrum—she seems to understand that right now I need comfort, and the warmth and solidness of Rowan and Mabel leaning on me, and Cinder patting my head, trickle heat into my body.

That, and the hot water is still blasting in the shower. Rowan sees me looking at it and reaches behind me to turn it off. Then he rests his hand on my shoulder, and when I don't resist, he puts his arm around me and pulls me into him.

"I'm sorry. I'm so sorry," I mumble. Blotches of tears mar his shirt, but he just rubs one warm, solid hand against my back. My hands clutch at Mabel's fur, and she wiggles until she's happily sitting across both our laps, her head on my elbow.

"*I'm* sorry," Rowan says. "I should have realized that these memories would be uncomfortable for you. If you want … I can do the rest on my own."

"No," I say adamantly, looking up at him with as much resolution as I can currently muster. "This is *my* spell. *My* family. I just … Give me a second. I'm kind of reliving the worst day of my life here."

His arm tightens around me, like he can protect me from my memories. And it almost works.

By the time dusk falls, we've gone through a number of books in my closet, but none of them contains anything pertaining to Egyptian spells. The work soothes me, and after I've washed my face, there are no more tears.

We stop around dinnertime. Rowan has run back to his aunt's to grab his laptop and a change of clothes, and gotten delayed filling her in on what happened.

"I gave her some of the details. I left out the part where I stayed over here last night," he says sheepishly. He hands me two large paper bags filled with Chinese takeout.

"If you got egg rolls, I forgive you," I say.

Fortunately for him, he did indeed get egg rolls.

We spread out the food and our notes and books on the kitchen table. I've just taken a gigantic bite of Kung Pao chicken when a video call comes across Rowan's laptop.

"It's Thad," he says, leaning over and accepting the call, then adjusting the screen so the caller can see us both.

Thad—Dr. Thaddeus Hallowell, museum curator and historian at Hawthorne College and senior member of the American Society for Ley Studies—appears onscreen. He's an older warlock, with neat silver hair and deeply tanned skin. He wears a button-up shirt under a knitted vest, and silver-rimmed glasses. He gives the appearance of someone who enjoys outdoor activities like polo and skiing.

"Rowan! Can you hear me?" Thad asks, adjusting his screen a few times.

"I can hear and see you fine," Rowan replies. Then he puts an arm casually around my shoulders. "Thad, this is Ivy Winthrop. The thread witch who's been helping me."

"Ah, Ivy! I've heard so much about you," Thad says, winking at Rowan. "She's even prettier than you said."

"Thad!" Rowan says, flushing. He rubs a hand across his face, like he's trying to conceal a smile. "Have you found anything about the Nekhbet prayer?"

"Ah. Yes," Thad says, and he pulls up a pile of ancient books, the stack so high I can barely see his silver hair over the top.

"Marta says hello, by the way," Thad says, riffling through a few pages. "She wants to know when you're coming over for dinner."

"Thad's wife," Rowan tells me. Then he turns back to the screen. "Soon. I promise."

Soon. He plans to be back at Hawthorne soon. I don't know why, but the idea makes my chest ache. Before I can think about it too much, a small stack of books topples, and Thad goes down with it.

"Oops!" he says, grabbing at the books with both hands. As he picks them up from the floor, he disappears from the screen for a second. "As you know, Nekhbet was an early deity, predynastic. No one's prayed to her for over two thousand years. I'm surprised the goddess even listens to that name anymore." Thad's voice is somewhat muffled under the desk.

He finally sits up and grabs a book from the center of the stack, the top ones swaying precariously—though they don't fall this time.

"Thad has a theory about all the ancient Egyptian and Celtic gods being facets of our goddess," Rowan explains. "Same magic, different names."

"Yes, well, it's not quite a theory. I'd call it a … hypothesis, perhaps. Or a postulation. Did you know that—"

"Did you find anything on how to reverse or undo an oracular amuletic decree?" Rowan interrupts. He mutes the laptop's microphone momentarily and whispers to me, "He'll keep going all day if I don't keep him on track."

"You know I'm a proficient lip-reader as well, my boy," Thad responds cheerfully, his smiling face peeking around the stack of books before him. "And don't think I've forgiven you for destroying the aetherometer, because I haven't."

"Anything on the decree, Thad?" Rowan repeats.

"Oh. Um, no. Sorry," he mumbles. "There might be something here, but you know we don't have all the ancient texts digitalized yet, and my assistant insists on staying in Fairhaven instead of continuing his research in Boston, like a civilized word warlock."

Rowan sighs, running a hand through his curls. It makes them stand up at all angles, and I fight the strangest urge to straighten them.

"I will say this, though," Thad says, his gaze fixed on me. "This spell? The one that bound your illness? Given the temporal relationship with the disappearance of magic from Fairhaven, it appears that the magic of your town was bound, as well."

I let out a long breath. He's given voice to the source of my deepest fear, my most gut-wrenching guilt. It *is* my fault. In saving me, my parents doomed our town.

"Hawthorne has the most extensive witch library in the Americas," Rowan says firmly. "It could take a while, but if there's an answer there, we'll find it."

"We?" Thad asks, eyebrows rising. "Are you coming back, then?"

I go still.

"Would you mind if I bring help?" Rowan asks, and he looks at me.

"Me?" I squeak. Go to Hawthorne College? *Leave* Fairhaven? Go *with Rowan?*

"Sure. You know more about this than either of us," he says matter-of-factly. "Three heads are better than two."

"I'll let the headmaster know to expect you both. How's tomorrow?" Thad asks.

My chest squeezes.

"Can you leave your shop for a few days?" Rowan asks.

"A few," I say, before I panic and my brain shuts down completely. "Most of my business is done online. I can bring a few projects to do on the drive."

I can't believe I said that. I can't believe I'm *considering* this.

"Great. We'll see you soon," Rowan says.

Thad mumbles an agreement, searching for the "end call" button on his laptop. Rowan smiles and closes the screen.

"Well? How about a road trip?" he asks.

I look into his blue eyes, so earnest and open. "How big is your car?"

CHAPTER 16

"A few days" away means I've got to pack my makeup and hair tools, plus Cinder's food and favorite toys, not to mention my mother's grimoire. Plus some stuff for work—I settle on the dress I'm making Ruby for her claiming party. She wants red, and sparkles. Like rubies. She's a beautiful girl, and on her special day, she's going to sparkle like a gem herself. And then there are *my* clothes. Oh, so many clothes. What if it's cold? What if I want to dress up? What if everyone there wears black all the time? Maybe I should bring some more traditional garb, just in case.

"Granny?" I call.

Granny has been strangely quiet since yesterday. In fact, I haven't seen her all day. I wonder if she's off on her own mission, or if she's found someone else to pester for a while.

"We'll be back soon," I tell Marvin as I set my suitcases by the front door.

He strains his branches toward me, like he wants to come.

"No. The college is no place for sentient mistletoe. All the hormones of college kids? You'd be going crazy," I chide.

Marvin ruffles his leaves innocently.

"Just try not to flood the apartment or anything while I'm gone."

Marvin gives me a gesture almost like a salute, then plops himself on the windowsill above the sink, where the morning light hits best.

"Granny?" I try again.

No answer.

Well, that's weird.

I open the apartment door, intending to start carting my luggage down, and run right into Rowan.

"Um, hi," he says. He's wearing a black crewneck sweater and jeans, and with his glasses, he looks every inch the modern warlock professor.

"Hi," I say.

He looks at my bags, and if he's concerned about the sheer number, he doesn't say anything.

"Is this all?" he asks. "I was prepared to cast a charm on my car like Mary Poppins's handbag."

I laugh. "Is that a real spell?"

We grab my bags, lock up, and head down the narrow stairs.

In my storefront window is a hastily scribbled *Out of town. Be back soon!*

"Not that I know of," he admits. "I could try, though."

Rowan drives a large black Volvo SUV that easily fits my bags in the trunk, nestled beside his single suitcase.

"That's all you packed?" I ask, one hand on my chest.

It's his turn to laugh. "Well, I'm kind of going home, you know? I was only visiting here. All my stuff is back in Boston."

He's only visiting here, I echo in my head.

"Right," I say.

I'm glad I wore my long wool coat today—there's a cold bite in the air. Cinder likes this coat too, because I lined the pockets in flannel, her favorite. She prefers the breast pocket, so she can see what's going on.

Mabel is in the back seat, her tail wagging hard in greeting. Rowan opens the passenger door for me, and when I slide in, I notice two cups from Song's Coffee Shop in the cupholders.

"It's about a two-hour drive," Rowan says. "I thought you might want something for the road."

Goddess, he's too thoughtful. *He's only visiting*, I remind myself. *Don't let yourself feel anything.*

The sweet pumpkin spice latte, however, starts to thaw my ice-cold heart.

We turn down Main Street and take the two-lane road east and out of town. We pass Farmer Brown's fields and his big red barn and the weathered colonial homes. I point out the small forest just outside town where Marigold lives in her cabin; we can just see the start of her beehives from the road.

We pass the wide silvered surface of the Quabbin Reservoir, then old white boarded churches and quaint mills along the river. We take Route 9 into Boston, passing gas stations and strip malls and a million coffee shops. Hawthorne College, Rowan reminds me as he takes an exit, is in a suburb called Wellesley.

There are several other schools in the area, so Hawthorne College doesn't stand out much there. There's even a legend that it was built on a plot of land granted to the Concord by Horatio Hollis Hunnewell himself, a major benefactor of Wellesley. And with a name like that, Rowan argues with a grin, it is likely Horatio was a warlock himself, though the history books apparently vary on the subject. On clear days, there seems to be a glow surrounding the school, which locals attribute to humidity or glare, when in reality it's a massive protection spell cast hundreds of years ago, and tied to the crossing of ley lines here.

Rowan likes to listen to instrumental music. Some of it is movie soundtracks; some of it is Broadway. He offers to let me pick the music, but I'm enjoying it, especially when he hums along. We reach Hawthorne College just after lunch, and I've made some decent progress on Ruby's dress. We stopped at a cute little diner for sandwiches. It's strangely and terrifyingly easy, just being with him.

It's a beautiful fall afternoon as we enter Wellesley. Big brick homes sit back from the main road, surrounded by old stone walls and iron gates. Huge elm and maple trees line the streets of the upscale neighborhood, bright red and orange and gold leaves dusting the sidewalks. A few pumpkins still decorate porches, and the air smells like cinnamon and fallen leaves. The town hall is a gorgeous old Victorian building with turrets that remind me of a castle.

Rowan slows and turns into a short road with a gated entrance. To either side of us, tall brick walls covered with sunset-colored ivy stretch as far as I can see, enclosing the college. On the outside, it looks like a classic New England preparatory school, with just a hint of Gothic architecture in the black steel gates and the arched windows of the buildings. A guard checks Rowan's ID, then looks sternly at me.

"Dr. Hallowell knows we're both coming," Rowan says.

The man frowns and steps back into his booth. He makes a quick phone call, looking back at us suspiciously a few times, before finally opening the gate.

"We take security very seriously here," Rowan says. "The neighbors think we're a prep school for wealthy families. I think there's a rumor we're secretly a psychiatric facility."

I laugh, and we're finally waved through the gate.

I get my first look at Hawthorne College. Two big elm trees guard the drive past the gate, and then there's a brick-and-glass greenhouse on my left, the Botanical Conservatory, a big building that looks like a mansion to my right, the Gravesend Dormitories, and then a large brick building with *Ashwell Library* inscribed over the massive archway. A few students drift out of the library—a witch in classic witchy black with a pointy hat, and a warlock with spiky neon-pink hair. They're talking animatedly about something as we pull up, their familiars—two cats, one black and one orange-striped—walking ahead of them, pretending to ignore each other.

In front of the library is the Founders' Green, an immaculately manicured lawn that Mabel promptly pees on with a delighted expression on her face.

A man is sitting at a little black bistro table to the side of the library, and he greets us with a wide smile. He tucks a thick book under his arm. He's wearing a tweed jacket with leather elbow patches over a button-up and khaki pants, a pair of glasses folded into his chest pocket. His silver hair is neatly combed, and his socks, I note, are bright orange. I like him immediately.

"Rowan! Ivy! So glad to see you," he says, embracing Rowan warmly. Thad shakes my hand, dark eyes twinkling. "So, young lady, ready to get to work?"

I clutch my mother's grimoire to my chest and manage a nod.

"You'll stay with my wife and me while you're visiting, of course,"

Thad says as we head into the building. "We have the guest room all prepared. Unless you've made other arrangements?"

"No. That will be lovely. Thank you," I manage.

Rowan makes a sound of protest beside me, and Thad raises an eyebrow.

"Unless you'd prefer to stay with Rowan, of course. I don't mean to presume," Thad says, eyes twinkling.

"Oh, no," I say, my face heating. "I'm not … that is, we're not …"

"Just watch out for Marta's familiar. She's a raven," Rowan warns, changing the subject quickly. "Keep your suitcase locked."

"Ah, yes," Thad acknowledges with a shrug. "There is that."

My face is still warm—did I assume I'd be staying with Rowan in his apartment here? I am honestly considering asking where the nearest pet-friendly hotel is—but then we enter the library, and my spinning thoughts fall still.

The inside of the library is immense, with huge vaulted ceilings and a glass dome up top. There are miles of bookcases, and apparently, several more floors below us. It's stunning, gorgeous, like something from an Ivy League campus. I feel very, very out of place. A sleek black cat with glowing yellow eyes greets us at the library counter.

"This is my familiar, Jeff," Thad says.

The cat rubs his head against Thad's hand and gives him a little trill of greeting. Then Jeff sniffs the air, like he can sense Cinder in my pocket. His tail swishes as he looks me over. Mabel comes to sit beside me, like a fluffy sentinel doing her best to protect my mouse. She eyes the cat thoughtfully.

"Um, has Jeff ever eaten another familiar?" I ask uneasily.

Thad puts a hand on his chest, offended. "Certainly not! We are a pair of well-behaved gentlemen."

Cinder peeks out of my coat pocket and squeaks at Thad. He gushes over her for a minute, Jeff's tail switching—but the cat doesn't make any attempt to eat my mouse. That's a good start.

"Well, what have we here?" Thad says, putting his glasses on and bending to take a closer look at my mouse. "I haven't seen a familiar of the *Mus musculus* variety in ages. Never could understand why. Smart creatures, mice."

Cinder gives a squeak of agreement.

"Very good. Well. Egyptian history is down this way," Thad says, gesturing ahead of us.

We descend a set of stairs into a darker but still-grand basement, past rows and rows of wooden bookshelves and tables and chairs, and once, we pass a pair of students making out. Thad clears his throat loudly, and they scurry off. I smother a snort of laughter.

Rowan takes this opportunity to tell Thad about Marvin, my sentient matchmaking mistletoe. I think of him as *"my* mistletoe" because even though Stella made him, well, he's mine for now, and apparently, he is happy with our arrangement—I will not admit that he's growing on me. Thad finds Marvin fascinating.

"You say he throws berries at you?" Thad asks, regarding me and pushing his glasses back up his nose. I nod.

"He's got good aim, too," I lament. Thad chuckles.

"I hate to tell you this," he starts. "But your mistletoe – 'he' is actually a 'she.'"

I stumble over nothing and barely catch myself from falling by grabbing the nearest bookshelf.

"Marvin? Marvin's a girl?" I ask, then laugh. "I figured if anything he was, um, asexual?"

"A trans-plant, perhaps," Rowan adds helpfully, steadying me as I stand, and I can't help another snort of laughter that escapes me. *Oh, Stella is going to* love *this!*

"You see, only the female plants have berries," Thad explains. "The male plants do not. Mistletoe is dioecious, though both sexes produce flowers."

I'm still pondering whether I should change Marvin's name when we round a corner to the Egyptian section of the library. I can tell because there is a big arch over two of the bookcases, helpfully labeling the section.

"The more common volumes are here," Thad says, patting the

nearest bookshelf fondly. "I thought we could start with these, then move on to the rare-volumes section."

There are hundreds of books before us. Thad must recognize the despair on my face, because he pats my arm reassuringly.

"Don't worry," he says. "We have the finest collection—"

"In the Americas," Rowan finishes for him.

Thad grins. "Yes! I was just going to say that! We'll have what you're looking for, never fear."

Thad finds us a table and some chairs, and I reluctantly hand him my mother's grimoire. He accepts it as gently as if it was made of glass.

"I shall take good care of it," he promises. "I'm a word warlock. Books—especially grimoires—are sacred to me."

Rowan steers me toward the bookshelves. I start at one end; he starts at the other.

"Just grab anything that looks promising," Rowan calls.

"*Shh!*" Thad says. "This *is* a library! Have you no sense?"

CHAPTER 17

It's approximately a thousand hours later. My eyes feel like they have sand in them, and my stomach is growling. Loudly. And my heart is getting heavier with disappointment by the minute.

"It may be time to take a break," Thad says. He's read my mother's grimoire carefully from cover to cover, taking notes as he went. Well, his spelled pen did, anyway. He uses a beautiful glass calligraphy pen with vibrant blue ink that writes as he whispers.

I close my copy of *Shadows of the Ebers Papyrus: Healing and Hexing in Ancient Egypt* and stretch my arms. Jeff has been sleeping all afternoon stretched out in the center of our table, which is slightly inconvenient. Mabel is getting antsy, though, walking around the floor, looking for someone to play with. I feel myself sympathizing with her.

Rowan started with a translated copy of the Ebers Papyrus and then read at least a dozen more. He's the fastest reader I've ever seen now that he's using his magic, and I'm guilty of watching him read nearly as much as I actually read myself. Guess that comes with the territory of his word magic.

"We should try the rare-book section tomorrow," Rowan says as we reshelve our books. "I can't imagine there's anything else here that would be of use."

"Agreed," Thad says cheerily.

The campus is dark, with flickering lanterns suspended in the elms, and jack-o'-lanterns of every shape and size glittering along the walkways. Thad and his wife, Marta, live behind the chapel, in the apartments set aside for faculty.

"They call the building a chapel and bell tower because that's what the early colonials were familiar with, of course, and so that's the way they designed and built it," Thad tells me as we walk. "In function, it's a temple. But we call it a chapel out of tradition."

The air is cool, and I pull my coat tight around me. Rowan is quiet and thoughtful as we walk, his gaze distant. In contrast, my head nearly swivels off my neck as I look around at the school—what would it have been like, learning here? Spending warm autumn evenings on the green with other students, doing research papers in the magical library, in a place where everyone is accepted and protected? An ache starts in my chest, and I rub my sternum absently, which doesn't really help.

The apartments are actually a row of quaint brick town houses, with iron lampposts and gates at each. Thad leads us to one with a neat garden of herbs out front. Jeff races past us when the door opens, eager to be home. Light and music and laughter pour out of the doorway, and I see Rowan's shoulders relax a little, a smile pull on his tired face.

Marta, it turns out, is a joyful Italian food witch. No wonder Rowan likes her so much, I think, as she piles our plates high with spaghetti and chicken breast and broccoli. Her raven, Misty, is better behaved than I expected, and other than occasionally snagging a piece of garlic bread from the bread basket, she mostly stays out of the way. Marta and Thad are delightful storytellers, and they love to hear about Fairhaven and my coven.

"So you have a food witch friend?" Marta asks, hands clasped as she gasps in excitement. "What is her name? I must meet her!"

"Her name is Marigold," I say, taking a sip of wine from my glass.

Their kitchen is small, and the four of us are crowded tightly around the round table, and the energy is warm and happy—and slightly tipsy.

"She owns a bakery in Fairhaven. She's the most amazing baker you'll ever meet," I say.

Marta insists that I give her Marigold's phone number immediately, which I do. Marta gushes over this tidbit as she types the information into her phone.

"Oh, another food witch! I'm so excited! We're not that common anymore," she says. "It'll be nice to have someone to exchange spells with! Most of my family is still in Italy, you know."

"My granny—well, the ghost of my great-great-something-grand-mother—would love to meet you too," I say, frowning a little when I remember how I haven't actually seen Granny in a while. "She got a spaghetti sauce recipe from an Italian witch generations ago and swears it's actually a love potion."

"Ah, love and food. My two favorite things," Thad says, patting Marta's hand fondly.

Marta blushes but leans over to give him a quick kiss.

The evening passes in a haze of laughter and wine and tiramisu. Eventually Marta notices Rowan yawning and insists we all go to bed immediately.

"Research is tiring work," she says.

Thad pats his belly and agrees.

"Can I help you clean up?" I offer, standing to put my dishes in the sink.

Marta smiles, patting my arm. "I forget you're not used to having magic around," she says. She waves her hand, and the dishes *fly* to the sink. The sponge and dish soap get to work all by themselves, in what appears to be a very well-choreographed spell.

"Well, that's convenient," I murmur, astounded at the casual use of magic. "Marigold will *definitely* want to know about that."

I mention my bags to Thad, which are still in the back of Rowan's car, and he waves his hand dismissively.

"I had them sent over while we were in the library. They're all in the guest room for you," he says. "Top of the stairs, then a right. Bath-room's in the hall. We'll start promptly at eight tomorrow." He glances at Rowan, who nods absently.

Marta rolls her eyes. "Thad won't even be awake before eight thir-ty," she whispers to me.

I thank them—Marta insists on a hug—and walk Rowan and Mabel to the door. Despite not finding anything helpful at the library today, I feel more hopeful than I have in ages. It probably has to do with the delicious food—and wine—in my belly, and of course, Marta and Thad's company. Cinder is completely passed out in my pocket, her little belly bulging with Marta's cooking. Other than Stella and her family, Granny, and sometimes Marigold, we don't spend time like this with other people much anymore. It's nice.

I'm thinking so much about this, and not about the placement of my feet, that when Rowan turns at the door to say goodbye, I run into him and nearly stumble.

"Whoa there," he says, lightly grabbing me by the shoulders and keeping me upright.

"Oh," I say, flushing, and I decide to blame the alcohol. "Um, sorry. I don't usually drink."

His hands are still on my shoulders, his eyes bright. I'm acutely aware of how very close we are, and my breath catches, my eyes flicking to his lips, which are so, so close. *I should kiss him*, I think—I also decide to blame this thought on the alcohol. And I suddenly, *desperately*, want to kiss him.

But before I can move, Rowan steps back, his hands leaving my shoulders quickly.

"Um, I'd be careful on the stairs, then," he says, rubbing the back of his neck. "I'll, um, see you in the morning."

He opens the door and lets Mabel out, and as he steps out into the night, he turns back once, his eyes finding mine.

And then he's gone, fading into the black night, like he was never even there at all.

CHAPTER 18

I awake the next morning to the glorious smells of bacon and coffee, and when I open the door of my room—after eight, as instructed—I am greeted by Marta's lovely singing voice. I change into jeans and a cream sweater and head downstairs. Cinder is already down there, being fed bits of pancake by Thad.

"Good morning! I hope my singing didn't wake you. I just love to sing!" Marta says, giving the last word a trill.

"No. It was the wonderful smells coming from your kitchen!" I say sincerely.

Marta beams, handing me a mug and directing me to the coffee pot. She's even got little pitchers of cream and a little bowl of sugar waiting.

I join Cinder and Thad at the table. Jeff is nowhere to be seen, but Misty is perched on a stand in the corner, eyeing me—or, more likely, the dangling moon-and-stars earrings I'm wearing.

"Sleep well?" Thad asks.

Marta gives me a plate piled high with pancakes and bacon and berries and tells me to dig in.

Well, I'd be an awful guest to deny her.

"Very well," I say. I leave out the part where a pair of ice-blue eyes haunted my dreams.

"You're nicer than the last one," Marta says, assessing me over the rim of her coffee mug.

I choke on a bit of pancake, and it takes a minute for my voice to return.

"Um, who are you talking about?" I ask, though I've got a pretty good idea.

Thad is completely immersed in a newspaper and gives no indication that he hears Marta.

"Laurel. His last girlfriend," Marta says. No need to ask who "he" is.

"Um, I'm not … we're not …" I try, my face flushing.

"Mm-hmm," Marta hums knowingly.

I take a big bite of pancake so I don't have to talk.

"Anyway," Marta says. "After *years* of dating, she ran off with his older brother. Did you know? Quite the scandal. I don't think he's talked to either of them since."

Misty caws in agreement from her perch by the sink.

Oh. He mentioned a previous relationship briefly when we met for coffee that first time, but I never asked for details. He did mention it had been a while since he'd been on a date. I guess getting over this Laurel would have taken a while.

"Oh. I … didn't know," I say.

Marta nods, like she's not surprised Rowan didn't share this awful bit of his history with me.

Thad shoots a glance toward his wife but makes no attempt to intervene.

"His parents took his brother's side, you know," Marta continues. "He hasn't talked to *them* in ages either. Spends most of his holidays with Thad and me now."

I stare into the dregs of my coffee cup, stomach churning a little with the knowledge.

"I hope they can make up someday," I say, meeting Marta's eyes.

She arches an eyebrow at me.

"I … I just know that I'd give anything to have one more day with my family," I say, a knot forming in my throat.

Marta reaches across the table and takes my hand, squeezing it firmly and giving me a warm smile. We finish our breakfast in silent communion, each of us, I think, having learned something vital already today.

Once my stomach is bulging and my blood is buzzing from caffeine, I get a text from Rowan.

"He's already at the rare-book section," I tell Thad.

Thad nods, like he's not surprised, and immediately gets up and grabs his shoes.

"Thank you, love," he says, giving Marta a kiss on the cheek.

She turns red and swats him with a towel.

"Go on, then," she says to us. "I'll send lunch over to the library for you."

I take a moment to fix my hair and apply some makeup—for no reason in particular—and grab my mother's grimoire. Cinder takes her place in my pocket, and we're off.

It is a gorgeous fall morning on campus, with tunnels of golden elm and flame-red maple trees lining every path. I can't help feeling, though, that it seems more … expansive than I initially thought.

"Oh, the wall?" Thad asks, tracing my gaze. "Yes. Fascinating bit of magic there. We have a modest plot for the school, but you'll find it is, as they say, bigger on the inside."

"Is it only witches here?" I ask as we pass the chapel and the green. The last of the leaves on the trees rustle softly as we pass. There's a chill in the air, though the early-morning sun on my skin promises that the day will be warm. We pass a few other witches and a warlock, their familiars dashing around—mostly cats, but also two foxes, a sleepy owl, and three more ravens.

"Only witches here," Thad confirms. "The vampires have their own facility in New York. I believe the werewolves have a place in Montana, but they're very secretive about it. The others, well, it would take me ages to list them all. We all have exchange students, of course, and I've been to the library at the vampire academy more times than I can count." He smiles. "We're very collegial."

I didn't know there were so many other supernaturals. We have a small family of werewolves nearby in Fairhaven, and once had some vampires visit, but that is it. I didn't imagine there were so many supernaturals in the world.

"Marta has a fondness for the faeries, of course," he continues. "They mostly stay in the greenhouse. She helps with their vegetable patch and herb garden. Fascinating people, faeries." As a word warlock, he has read more books and accumulated more knowledge than any other ten witches I know—not to mention, he has access to the "largest collection of magical texts in the Americas," I think with a grin.

A thought occurs to me. All that knowledge, and he still doesn't know about how I can fix Fairhaven's magic? A worrisome pit forms in my stomach, which I don't think I can blame on Marta's amazing cooking. I'm silent as we enter the library, gripping my mother's grimoire like a shield before me.

There's a room at the back of the first floor of the library that I didn't notice before. It's got large wooden doors with runes and wards in different languages carved into them—it looks like a mixture of Celtic, Egyptian, and maybe Norse. Thad opens the doors, and as my fingers touch them, a jolt of magic races up my arms.

"What was *that*?" I whisper.

"Protective spells. Keeps out anyone with unpure motives, or any non-witches," Thad explains. I swallow. Well, my motives towards the *books* are pure, anyway.

Inside the rare-book room are rows of dark wooden tables set between a few large bookshelves. The majority of the books are on the perimeter of the room, extending from the floor to the very high vaulted ceiling, reachable by rolling ladders. Above us, arched Gothic windows with iron latticework filter in sunlight. Green-shaded lamps illuminate even the darkest corners of the room with a soft glow. It's quiet. As quiet as a tomb.

"There are runes on the windows to protect the oldest works here from the sun," Thad explains. "The air, you'll notice, is purified, and the humidity in here is strictly controlled. And"—he hands me a pair of white cotton gloves—"you'll need to wear these when touching anything. Some of the books will set off an alarm if you touch them with bare skin."

I nod, a little overwhelmed. My eyes immediately find Rowan, bent over a stack of books already. The morning light turns his hair bright gold. He's wearing a black wool blazer over a black shirt and looks … comfortable. At home. *He belongs here*, I think. It suits him. *He belongs* here. *Not in Fairhaven.* The thought makes the knot in my stomach squeeze harder. I swallow, which doesn't help, and try to put a smile on my face.

We join him and get to work. He's immersed in the books. If last night's almost-kiss caused him any anxiety, he's not showing it. Judging by the pile of notes already spread before him, he's been here a while already. Maybe hours. *Then again, he was here very early. Trouble sleeping, I wonder?*

My chest squeezes—I know that helping Fairhaven, researching the ley lines, is part of his job, and his research. But he's helping me too.

I decide to start with a large, thin tome bound in what seems to be crocodile skin. *Sorcery and Spells on the Nile*, by T. A. Wright. Rowan and Thad flip through the volumes with astounding speed. And when they finish the pile, they return the books and go back for more.

The rare books are fascinating. I swear some of them have titles that shift when I look at them directly. Some are bound with a chain and a lock, as if the book itself was dangerous, not only for the material within. One even seems to pulse gently, as if *breathing*.

We break around noon for lunch, which Marta has sent to the library in a floating picnic basket. We stretch and enjoy the autumn sunshine at the black metal bistro tables out front. Marta made massive sandwiches, piled high with meat and cheese and peppers. She even sent some dried-beef snacks for Jeff and Mabel, and berries for Cinder. Big flasks full of sweet tea soothe our parched throats— the air in the rare-book room is very dry.

I text Stella, letting her know we haven't found anything yet. She tells me that Ruby is sick again, and that she's being sent to Philadelphia for some testing. I can tell even from the way she types that she's worried. *I should be there for her.* I resolve to find the answer to Fairhaven's ley lines, *quickly*, and get back to my friend and my niece. *If we can restore magic, she can use it to help Ruby.* Then I frown, because this is exactly what got us into trouble in the first place. *She's going to be fine.* It's the closest I've come to praying to the goddess in ages. *She will be fine.*

But a trickle of dread coils tight inside my chest, like a snake poised to strike, and won't leave.

"Marta runs the kitchens on campus most days of the week," Thad explains, and I shake my head to clear my heavy thoughts and try to pay attention to him. "She also teaches cooking for noncooking witches a few times a month. It's one of the more popular classes."

"I can't imagine why," I say, mouth full of the best brownie I've ever had in my *life*. Maybe I should ask Marta if I can bring some home to Ruby. She'd love these.

We return to the library. Thad takes an armful of books to be reshelved. I sit on the table, legs dangling, feeling a little discouraged. Two word warlocks, the most comprehensive magical library ever, and we still haven't found anything that might counteract the spell my parents cast.

"You okay?" Rowan asks, shutting the book he has been reading and coming over to me.

"Just feeling a little down … Do you really think the answer is here?" I ask.

He frowns. "It has to be," he says confidently. "But if it's not, well, I suppose we could try Cairo next."

I hold back a laugh. It feels sacrilegious in this place.

"Yes, I suppose that is the next logical step," I tease.

"Don't worry," he says, coming closer, so that he's nearly touching my knees. "We'll find the answer."

I look up at him. Even though I'm seated on the table, he's taller than me. There's an earnestness in his expression, and a kind of resoluteness. And goddess help me, but I trust him.

He swallows and steps closer, hands brushing my knees.

"Ask me," he says, voice low. The air between us feels suddenly charged.

"What?" I ask, and my own voice has gone suddenly breathless.

"I promised you I wouldn't flirt with you again until you asked me to," he says, his hands making the skin on my thighs tingle. "For the love of the goddess, *ask* me. When you're sitting here like this, looking so lost, it makes me want to take you in my arms and ki—"

"There you two are!" Thad says, with the absolute *worst* timing. "I think I've found something! Come on!"

"We should probably, um …" I bite my lip and glance toward Thad.

Rowan's eyes flicker to my mouth and back up—then he steps back slowly, as if it takes an extraordinary amount of effort. The air rushes back into my lungs.

"Yes," Rowan agrees. He offers his hand, and I take it to jump down from the table.

But he doesn't let it go while we make our way back to Thad and the stack of books.

"What have you found?" Rowan asks.

Thad excitedly holds up the book he's reading—*The Eye of Ra*.

"It's a series of curses and countercurses in ancient Egypt," he says quickly. "Based on the worship of Sekhmet."

"Egyptian goddess of healing," Rowan explains.

I nod, and we crowd around Thad as he reads. It's possibly the most exciting lead we've had yet, though I'm finding myself distracted by the warm, solid presence beside me.

"It seems that lifting a spell and lifting a curse are essentially the same," Thad says, pointing to a chapter in the book.

"What language is that?" I ask, frowning.

"That's hieratic," Rowan says, his shoulder brushing mine. "A kind of shorthand of hieroglyphics used by the priests. Tricky to translate, but we've had lots of practice. Give us a few minutes?"

Rowan and Thad bend their heads together over the book, both writing notes frantically, crossing things out and whispering their arguments. I bite my lip and try not to look as anxious as I feel. I pace the library, returning books to—hopefully—their rightful places. One book *wiggles* when I try to shelve it, and I realize I've misplaced it. When I finally find its correct spot, it gives a sigh and settles down. Magical books are wild. At least they keep me moderately distracted while Rowan and Thad work.

It takes longer than "a few minutes"—in my estimation, over an hour at least—but then they both leap up together, shaking a piece of paper in triumph. Hope floods my chest.

"Ivy, come see!" Rowan says, handing me the paper. "It invokes the Egyptian deities for help. We'll have to get a few things together ..."

"Water from the Nile?" I read, my hope fading, like water spilling from a broken cup. "A lotus flower?" Do we really have to go all the way to Cairo after all?

"We can substitute local river water for the Nile, never fear," Thad says. "I've done it many times. And I'm fairly sure we can still find lotuses in the botanical gardens, if the faeries haven't picked them all."

The thought of actually lifting the spell—not to mention visiting the gardens and seeing *real faeries*—has me feeling a little lightheaded.

"Curse-breaking in Egyptian is largely formulaic," Thad explains, scribbling a few more things. "You state the purity of intention, invoke the deities, banish *isfet*, and restore order."

"*Isfet?*" I ask, wrinkling my forehead.

"Chaos," Rowan explains. "Then there are some ritualistic actions to go along with the spoken words."

Then he starts to speak, reading from the book in front of us, in a language I've only heard once before.

And everything goes dark.

CHAPTER 19

"Ivy? IVY!"

Rowan's voice comes to me as if from a great distance, but when the fog in my vision clears, his face is only inches away. I blink, clearing my eyes—somehow I'm looking up at Rowan and … the ceiling? With its giant dark beams and Gothic windows? Cinder is sitting on my chest, chattering away at me, her whiskers twitching a mile a minute.

I push myself up—I must have fallen down.

Cinder grabs onto my sweater and continues her tirade, never letting up for a second.

"What happened?" I ask, my tongue feeling thick and clumsy in my mouth. I pass a hand over my face, my hair—I seem to be in one piece. Cinder finally pauses a moment to take a breath.

"You fainted," Rowan says, his own face white as a sheet.

I realize then that his hand is around my back, that he's holding me.

"Are you okay? Does anything hurt?"

I sit up, and Rowan's hands slip away from me. I feel a little dizzy, but otherwise fine.

"I don't know," I say, and when I move to stand, Thad and Rowan immediately jump to help me up and get me to a chair.

Cinder still clings to my sweater, refusing to let me go. Mabel comes and lays her warm head in my lap, licking my hand with her tongue.

"How do you feel?" Thad asks. He hands me a bottle of water, and I take a sip.

I don't *feel* bad at all. I can't even remember the last time I fainted or felt dizzy like this.

"I'm fine," I assure him. "I think maybe ... too much excitement?"

It seems plausible. I've never been away from Fairhaven for long. And all the wonderful things here at Hawthorne College have definitely overwhelmed me. My head, at least, is starting to clear a little. I'm just ... I've never fainted before. Or at least, not since I was sick as a child. This thought makes my brow furrow—despite the spell, has my cancer somehow returned? I haven't seen a doctor in ages—the town only has one, and he's not the friendliest person, but I vow to go get checked out when we get home.

This announcement, at least, settles Thad and Rowan a little. The men nod and immediately begin to close books and put things away.

"Let's get you some fresh air," Rowan says, taking my elbow and leading me from the library. He holds my mother's grimoire and our notes in his other hand.

By the time we're seated at the tables out front, I'm feeling completely like myself again.

"I'm so sorry for interrupting," I say, flushing. "That was ... unexpected."

Rowan frowns, thinking. I take a sip of water while he searches for the right words, running a hand through his curls.

"You fainted when I started reading the counterspell," he says. "Well, it's kind of a generic countercurse, but in theory, it should still work."

"You think it had something to do with the spell?" I ask, and now it's my turn to frown. Magic has never made me faint before. Made my expensive fancy underwear fly away, yes. But faint? Not so far.

"It's ... one possibility. Are you feeling at all feverish? Maybe you're getting sick. I should take you back to Fairhaven."

I lay a hand on his arm to stop him, and he immediately covers it with his other hand, eyes bright and serious.

"I'm fine. Really. I want to keep going. I mean, if you do."

"Of course I do," he says firmly, his hand still gripping mine. "I want to keep going. I want Fairhaven free of whatever is upsetting the magic. I want ... goddess, I want so many things."

Thad and Jeff come bounding out from the library before he can elaborate further. Jeff chooses a patch of sunlight on the warmed brick and cleans his paws, while Thad joins us at the table.

"How are you feeling? Better, I see. Oh, there they are. Can I see those?" Thad asks, gesturing for the papers in front of Rowan.

He reluctantly lets me go to pass them over.

Thad studies them for a minute before nodding emphatically and crossing something out, scribbling frantically.

"There," he says, speaking mostly to the papers. "I'm off to prepare the altar. Rowan, meet me in the chapel after you get the lotus. With any luck, we'll have this spell lifted and be home tonight in time for dinner."

"Can I come with you?" I ask Rowan.

"Are you sure you're feeling all right?" he asks gently.

I pat his hand in an attempt to be reassuring, and his fingers curl around mine.

"Never better," I assure him, warmth flooding my face. "Besides, this is all my fault, anyway. I should help fix it."

"None of this is your fault," Rowan says firmly, his jaw set. "None of it."

It's a sweet sentiment, even if it's not true.

Hand in hand, we leave Thad and make our way to the gardens. Rowan walks slowly, whether because he's aware my legs are much shorter than his or because he's still worried about me. Or maybe he just wants to prolong our time together.

I think about what he said, about the spell on Fairhaven not being my fault. It is. I mean, it's not my fault I got leukemia. That sucked, but it was just regular bad luck. But it was my parents' doom that they loved me so much that they did everything they could to protect me. I think of Stella and Ruby—goddess, I'd do anything for them. I under-stand why my parents did what they did, but it also means I now have a responsibility to save the rest of the town from it.

I just have to wonder if a fainting episode is going to be the worst of the repercussions.

Before I know it, we've crossed the campus and reached the green-house. The Botanical Conservatory looks like a large colonial brick home with a Gothic greenhouse attached to the right side. The front has a white cupola entrance, and the entire building is surrounded by manicured plants in riotous colors. Butterflies in iridescent shades flutter around like falling leaves.

We head right for a door into the greenhouse, and we're greeted by a witch in brown overalls with gardening implements shoved in every pocket and a pair of thick gloves in her hands.

"Rowan! Good to see you," she says, grinning widely and shaking his hand, then mine.

He introduces me to Dr. Hazel Elmstead, lead plant witch at Hawthorne. She has neat black braids pinned tightly in a bun and a wide bright smile. I like her immediately.

"Egyptian lotus? Of course! Follow me," she says. "The blue water lily, or *Nymphaea coerulea*, prefers full sun. And plenty of water, of course. We've got them over here."

Rowan makes Mabel wait outside. The dog pouts but sits where she's told to.

The inside of the greenhouse is dappled in light. I notice the same runes on the glass as are on the windows in the library—protection. Plants of all kinds form a maze of green from wall to wall, so it's impossible to see more than a few feet ahead. We follow Hazel through the maze to a small stone clearing near a corner of the building. A shaft of sunlight falls directly onto the stone pond in the center, in which float a dozen large lily pads crowned with blue flowers.

And dancing on the lily pads are a swarm of dragonflies—*Wait, no.* As we get closer, I see that these creatures are flying around upright, though they do have shimmering wings.

"Faeries," Rowan says, a smile on his face. "Mabel likes to chase them. Even tried to eat one once."

"So *that's* why you left her outside," I say with an answering smile.

"I didn't want to create an international supernatural incident because my dog ate a faerie," he says.

The faeries have noticed us, and a few fly over to see us. One hovers directly in front of me, so close I nearly need to cross my eyes to see her. She looks like the tiniest person I have ever seen, maybe two inches tall, with long brown hair in braids and a dress made of flower petals. Her skin is light purple and shimmers as if she's covered in glitter. She flies from side to side before my face, inspecting me. She says something, her voice so soft I can barely hear it.

"She's asking why you're here," Hazel says with a shrug. "I had to learn their language ages ago if I wanted to keep them from plucking all my best roses."

"Oh. Does she, um, I mean, do you …?" I say, redirecting my question at the beautiful faerie. "Do you understand me?"

The faerie nods.

"We're here to get a lotus to help lift a curse on my town," I say, which sounds frustratingly simple when I put it like that.

Her eyes widen, one hand flying to her mouth. She zips around, and the other faeries coalesce around her like a little glittering tornado. They drift across the pond and settle on the largest flower, a bright blue-and-purple lotus in full bloom, as if marking it for me.

"Here," Hazel says, handing me a pair of shears that look like they are made from silver. "Trim it as far down as you can. Just leave the shears when you're done." She waves at us and heads toward a group of witch students emerging from the greenery, herding them toward a bed of sunflowers that must be ten feet tall.

The faeries follow her like a swarm of butterflies, though the one I spoke to earlier stops by and rests a little hand on my cheek, like she's wishing me good luck.

Seeing the faeries is like … something out of a dream. A reminder that there is still plenty of magic in this world, and that it can be absolutely beautiful. My resolve to help Fairhaven hardens.

I look at the lotus flowers. They're as big as my hand, with bright blue petals and a purple-tipped yellow crown in the middle. They are exquisite, and it seems a shame to cut one.

"Just one?" I ask, bending toward the nearest, the big one that the faeries picked out.

"Just one," Rowan confirms.

I grab the stem, which is warm from the sun, and cut low, as Hazel instructed. I lay the shears on the edge of the shallow pond and stand, finding myself suddenly very alone with Rowan, with just the flower between us.

"Are you sure you're all right?" he asks. He raises his hand, hesitates, then brushes a strand of green hair back from my face, tucking it gently behind my ear.

"Fine," I whisper.

Why am I whispering? And is it suddenly hot in here?

"I don't suppose there's any chance of you going back to rest, and letting Thad and me finish the spell tonight?" Rowan asks, eyebrows knitted in concern.

I shake my head, which does not, apparently, surprise him.

"None," I say firmly.

He nods, but neither of us moves.

"Actually," I say, and I swallow hard before I can talk myself out of it. "There was something I wanted to ask you."

"Of course. Anything," Rowan says, a small smile on his face.

"Would you ... that is, I think I would like it, very much, if you would ... that is, *wouldyoupleaseflirtwithmeagain?*" I blurt out, my heart pounding.

Rowan nods for a moment, considering, and my stomach flips. Then he gently takes the lotus from my hand and sets it on the side of the pond by the shears.

"Um, don't we need that?" I ask, my brain clearly malfunctioning.

"It can wait," he says. He steps closer, his gentle hands finding either side of my face.

"Does this mean I need to tell Dahlia that her palmistry app worked?" I babble.

"I'll try to remember to thank her," Rowan says, his thumb tracing my bottom lip.

I swear that all rational thought completely leaves my body.

"Rowan?" I ask.

His breath stops, his eyes snapping to mine, like he's afraid I'm going to change my mind. "Yes?" His hands fall from my cheeks, landing lightly on my shoulders.

"What were you trying to say in the library? Before Thad inter-rupted?" I ask in a whisper.

"I'd wager you have a guess or two," he says, one corner of his mouth quirking up.

I grin. "I think you said … you wanted to kiss me."

"I think you're right," he says, relief softening his face.

"I think … I think I'd be all right with that," I say, before my courage fails.

Rowan's hands slip to my waist, pulling me up tight against him. I can't help the little gasp that escapes me, or the smile that curves my lips.

"*Finally,*" he breathes.

And then he kisses me.

I've been kissed before. But no one, *no one*, has made sparks light up my blood like Rowan Hale. I don't know if it's magic or Dahlia's "soulmates" thing or whatever, but I would swear in that moment that I was on fire. His kiss is earnest, and passionate, and I swear to the goddess if he wasn't holding me, I'd float right out of this greenhouse.

My hands have found themselves twined around his neck; his hand on the small of my back is pressing me into him.

"All right?" he asks after a moment, breathing a little hard. He leans his forehead against mine.

"All right," I say.

He smiles, outdazzling the sun, and gives me another quick kiss. Goddess, but I want more.

"If you kiss me again, I'm afraid we're going to be *very* late meeting up with Thad," I manage to say.

Rowan positively groans. "Don't tempt me, witch," he says. But he's smiling, and we leave the greenhouse with our hands linked, my heart full—and with one beautiful Egyptian lotus, which I've decided is my favorite flower from now on.

Thad is already in the chapel when we get there. The brick building has a large clock on the front, and a white bell tower extending high overhead. Inside, it has the setup of a church, with rows of pews, but the altar is in the center of the room instead of the front, and all the pews spread out concentrically like rays of the sun from it. Our footsteps on the stone floor echo around the chapel, and Thad looks up from his preparations to wave to us.

"I am thinking of trying the incantation in English," Thad says. If he notices that something has changed between Rowan and me, he doesn't say anything, though I can only imagine that the redness on our cheeks is like a giant flag. "There never seems to be a particular need for a certain language, and I'm much less likely to say something wrong in English."

"Good idea," Rowan says, clearing his throat.

We help Thad make a thin circle of sand around the altar, and stand inside it. It's early evening now, but we're alone in the chapel. It's dark and a little eerie. I wonder if Hawthorne College has ghosts—if I were a ghost, this is totally the kind of place I'd haunt. My skin prickles at the thought, and I miss Granny so much it almost hurts.

The altar is small and made of a single piece of gray stone that has clearly been here for a long, long time. Thad sets a shallow bowl of water on it and lights a small white candle.

"Good magic, pure words."

He sprinkles salt into the bowl. A rush fills my ears, like roaring water.

"Knowledge of the gods, sacred in power."

Thad gestures to me, and I hand him the lotus. He sets it into the bowl as well. My chest feels tight, like I can't take a deep breath, and my hands go cold. *Relax*, I tell myself. *It's just nerves. A few more minutes, and Fairhaven will be safe. Your home will be safe.*

Thad pulls a small loaf of bread I recognize as part of our lunch today from his pocket, with a wink in my direction. I try to give him a smile.

"An offering to Isis, and to Sekhmet."

He crumbles the bread onto the altar and pinches the flame on the candle, dousing it.

Beside me, Rowan takes my hand, but I barely feel it. I feel … lightheaded. As if I'm no longer connected to my body. As if …

"Let *isfet* be driven back. Let *ma'at* …"

And then—I don't feel anything at all.

CHAPTER 20

Darkness. Everything is dark. *Again.* My eyelids hurt and feel too heavy to open. There is a slight pressure on my chest, and my hands and legs won't move. *Am I dead?* No, I decide. Definitely not. I hurt too much to be dead.

With a herculean effort, I pry one eye open and see that I'm in what appears to be a hospital bed, with white sheets and white walls and a white ceiling. On my chest, the small weight I feel—a tiny sleeping mouse, curled up, guarding me as I recover from … whatever this is.

I turn my head to the side to find a white curtain drawn for privacy. To my other side, a sleeping man leans back in a small chair, blond stubble on his cheeks and a sleeping golden retriever at his feet.

Rowan. How long did I pass out for this time? It's still dark outside the windows, and my room is dark except for one small light on a side table.

My head is pounding, and my limbs feel leaden, but I manage to push myself up in bed. Cinder, my sweet Cinder, wakes and immediately runs to my shoulder, where she licks my cheek and squeaks a very agitated lecture into my ear. The noise wakes first Mabel and then Rowan. Mabel gets to her feet and comes over to put her paws on my bed and lick my hand, my arm, anything her warm, wet tongue can reach.

"Okay, Mabes. Let her rest," Rowan says, gently pulling the dog off the bed. He crouches by the bedside, blond curls all frizzed, like he's been running his hands through them all night.

I'd like to run my hands through them too.

"What happened?" I manage to croak.

Rowan takes a cup from the table and helps me drink. My arms are still incredibly weak, and I'd drop the cup if not for his assistance. What happened to me?

"You're in the hospital ward, a hall in the dormitories," Rowan explains. His face is gray, with dark circles under his dulled eyes. "You had a seizure. I've never been so … It was scary, to watch."

"A seizure? I've never had a seizure. I've actually never been sick a day since I got cured of the leukemia."

"I know," Rowan says wearily, passing a hand over his features.

"You know … what?" I ask.

"You told me once you rarely got sick. I'd say it was more likely never. Is that right?"

"I just said that," I say, confused. "I think … I wonder if maybe my leukemia could be coming back." I bite my lip.

Rowan shakes his head, and his confidence eases my heart a little.

"I think, somehow, your health is tied to this spell. The first time we tried to lift it, you fainted. The second time, you had a seizure." He looks at me, blue eyes intense. "I don't think we should try it a third time."

"What?" I exclaim. "You didn't finish the spell?"

He shakes his head.

"But if we don't lift it, the ley lines in Fairhaven are going to be stuck forever!" I sputter, trying to peel the blanket from my legs.

"And if we do lift the spell, you could die," Rowan says softly.

Cinder rustles gently on my shoulder, and I pet her absently.

"That's your opinion," I say, and yes, I'm fully aware of how petulant I sound.

"Thad's too," he says.

"Well … then we'll try something else," I say, gripping the covers tightly between my hands.

"What else?" Rowan asks.

"Anything else!" I fire back. Anything else. Everything else. I won't stop.

"We can't risk your life," Rowan says, crossing his arms. "I won't do it."

We glare at each other for a moment.

On the one hand, it's incredibly sweet that he's worried about me. On the other, he clearly doesn't understand how much lifting this spell, this curse, means to me.

"Let's go back home," I say after a minute.

"*This* is my home," Rowan reminds me, like a punch to my gut.

I swallow. *Right.* His home isn't in Fairhaven, isn't with me. Goddess, so what if we kissed one time? And all right, it was a fantastic, amazing kiss, and even though he's making me so mad right now, I would totally kiss him again. I swallow hard and try again, my voice squeaking a little.

"I meant, could you take me home, please?"

His face softens, and he takes my hand. "If that's what you want. You could … stay here awhile, if you wanted. We could keep looking."

A tug pulls at my heart, like a fishing line physically connecting me to Fairhaven. I've never been away for so long, and honestly, I think that might be part of the reason these strange things are happening to me. I know Rowan won't be staying, that he'll be coming back to Hawthorne to keep working on this spell with Thad—or worse, that he'll give up on us both, on me and the spell, and move on. The spell that can't be lifted, and the woman he can't stay with. He belongs here, and I belong in Fairhaven.

I take a deep breath.

"No," I say, resigned. "I think I'd like to go home."

"Granny? Marvin? I'm home," I call. I'm tired and aching like I have the flu, and it's all I can do to make my feet climb the stairs to my apartment.

Marvin greets me at the door, leaves rustling like he's in a tornado, branches high in the air. Or like "she's" in a tornado, I guess?

"Calm down, Marv. What's going on?" I ask, tabling the gender discussion for now.

Marvin uses his/her branches like crutches, or spider legs, running around my apartment, looking in every corner.

"Looking for something?" I ask, setting down my bags.

Rowan closes the door behind us. It was a quiet, awkward ride home, though I'm still sad it's over, because now it means less time to spend with Rowan. Marvin bobs up and down at my assessment of his antics—he's agreeing with me.

"Granny?" I call.

There's no answer.

Marvin bobs up and down again. I frown.

Granny, he's saying, is missing.

"Sometimes she disappears for a bit. She'll be back eventually," I say. I wonder if she got confused because I was in another city—I'm not exactly clear on how her ghostly tether to our family works.

Marvin shakes from side to side. He disagrees.

"Has she been gone a long time? The whole time I've been gone?" I ask.

He agrees again.

"Hmm," Rowan says.

"Hmm?" I ask.

I head for the cabinet, grab a glass, and fill it with water. I take a sip. My head feels foggy, which I guess is an aftereffect of the seizure. I rub my forehead, willing the sensation to ease a little.

"It's just … interesting. That's all," he says—but he's frowning, and there's a little V shape where his eyebrows come together. He's thinking about something.

"Well, thanks for dropping me off," I say, in as light a tone as I can manage.

We haven't kissed since the greenhouse, though the goddess knows I want to. I want to kiss him again and run my hands through those curls and take off his glasses and …

My thoughts go on and on, despite the fact that Rowan and I have barely spoken since I woke up from the seizure. I'm exhausted, and all I *should* want to do is take a shower and go to sleep. I have tons of orders I need to catch up on, and a bunch of online requests. Life needs to get back to normal. I'm certain Granny will show up, eventually.

Probably.

Then my phone rings—it's Stella.

"Hey, Stell—" I start, cradling the phone against my shoulder as I take my other bags from Rowan.

She's talking so fast I can't understand her. There's a lot of background noise, like wind—and is she crying?

"Stella? Stells? What's going on?" I ask.

I eventually catch the words "Ruby" and "sick." After that, it's a lot more crying.

"Hang on. Don't go anywhere. I'll be right there," I say, and hang up.

My heart is pounding. Sure, Ruby has had some colds this year, but this sounds serious. A lot more serious. Flashbacks of my own childhood spent in hospitals come to me—I know Stella and Jacque took Ruby into the city for some tests, but I haven't asked Stella how it all turned out. I curse myself for being a thoughtless friend and grab my keys.

I turn to head out and run smack into Rowan's chest.

"What's going on?" he asks.

"I'm not sure," I say, biting my lower lip. My eyes start prickling with unshed tears. Ruby is *family*. I can't stand the thought of anything bad happening to her. Any thoughts of my fatigue fly right out of my head. "Ruby's not doing well. Stella seems really upset."

Rowan nods and follows me out. We lock up and head back down to the street. I hold on to the stair rail more than I care to admit; my legs still feel heavy and clumsy.

And I can't help wondering … is the timing of Ruby getting sick somehow related to all this? To the ley lines acting up?

"I'll drive you over," Rowan says, and I'm too frazzled to do anything but accept.

Mabel is in the back seat of his SUV and wags her tail when she sees me coming back. From my hoodie, Cinder squeaks encouragingly.

We get to Stella's home in a few minutes. I race up the front stairs and go in without bothering to knock.

Stella's home is always spotless, done up in refined neutrals. I've always thought it looked like something from a magazine, or maybe a museum, with its crystal orbs and obelisks.

Today, though, with a pair of women in blue scrubs talking quietly and stacks of boxes and medical supplies by the door, it feels more like a hospital.

I spot Stella down the hall and make a beeline for her. She's talking to another woman in scrubs, but when she sees me, her face crumples, and she grabs me in a tight hug.

"What's going on?" I ask.

Stella sniffles and lets me go, but not very far. "Ruby. The tests … the doctors can't figure out what's wrong with her. She can't eat. Her fever won't break. Her blood … she's anemic. She's had transfusions, but they don't help. These women," she says, gesturing with a nod at the kind-looking lady behind her, "are with home health. They're here to … to make sure Ruby is comfortable. While we keep … keep …"

"Comfortable?" I echo, my chest cracking open. I feel more than hear Rowan come up behind me, a solid presence. I lean back a little on him as my world crashes down.

"We're going to keep trying, of course," Jacque says, coming up quietly behind Stella and resting a hand on her shoulder. "But … they've asked us to prepare. For the … for the worst."

Stella grabs Jacque's hand like it's a life preserver and she's drowning. This statement brings a roar of sound, and I can't tell if it's Stella wailing or me. We crumple to the floor in a heap, arms around each other, tears running down our faces.

Rowan brings us tissues, and in a few minutes, we manage to catch our breath, though we keep our hands tightly locked together. *Ruby. Little Ruby. My little gem. Goddess, no. This can't be happening. It can't.*

Rowan and Jacque have joined us on the kitchen floor. The nurses, thankfully, have headed upstairs to tend to Ruby.

After a little longer, Stella and I get up, unspoken resolution on our faces.

"Can I see her?" I ask.

Stella nods, her beautiful face puffy and pale from crying.

I squeeze her hand, and Rowan and I go upstairs. I do my best to wipe my smeared makeup off on my sleeve—it won't do for Ruby to see me looking like that.

Ruby's room has pink walls and piles of stuffed animals of all kinds—practice for when she's a vet someday, she always says. Despite her occasionally angsty teenage attitudes, she hasn't gotten rid of them.

Or at least, her room used to look like that. Today all her toys, all those memories, have been cleared out, likely stuffed into her closet, which is now closed instead of displaying her piles of clothes and dresses, many of which I made for her.

An IV goes into her upper arm with a thick fluid running through it.

And Ruby. *Oh, goddess, my Ruby.*

She's so pale, her usual golden glow now wan and faded. Her hair hangs in sweat-plastered strands across her face; her cheeks are sunken. Her chest rises and falls in a slow, steady rhythm, her eyes closed.

"She's sleeping," one of the nurses tells me with a kind smile. "I'll let her know you stopped by when she wakes."

I nod, a hand over my mouth to keep myself from screaming. This faded, skeletal figure before me isn't my niece. This isn't the girl who twirls in sparkly dresses and plucks feathers from her mother's macaw and makes dandelion crowns at Beltane. I can barely recognize her amid the blankets and IV poles and monitors around her, beeping softly, covering up the sound of her breathing.

By the time I compose myself and make it back down the stairs, Stella and Jacque are sitting at the kitchen table, each holding a full cup of coffee that neither is drinking. They are as still as statues, eyes open but unseeing.

I sit by Stella, and eventually she starts talking. Rowan stands behind me, tentatively putting a hand on my shoulder. I grab it, drawing strength from him, as Stella talks. I don't care anymore that he's going back to Hawthorne. I don't care that we had a fight, or whatever that was. He steadies me now, and I latch on to that steadiness with all my strength.

Stella tells me about all the tests they ran on Ruby in Philadelphia, about all the specialists they saw, the scans, and the medicines. Ruby just keeps wasting away. Aplastic anemia is the best diagnosis they've come up with, but she's too weak to undergo a bone marrow transplant.

"We have to talk to Hartwood," I say, looking up at Rowan.

He nods, his mouth drawn tight.

"I ... may have tried some spells," Stella says. "While we were in Philadelphia. Magic there isn't as strong as it used to be here, but ... it didn't help. I brought bags of crystals, rosemary, sage, lavender, yarrow. I couldn't burn incense in the hospital, of course, but I thought surely *something* ... and her claiming is supposed to be in two weeks. I was hoping, maybe, that ..."

"You did all you could," I say, which isn't as comforting as I hoped. I lean into Stella, wishing I could take this pain from her and from Ruby ...

Or can I?

"Have you tried your healing spells since you've been home?" I ask.

Stella looks at me, the anguish in her eyes clearing for a moment. "No."

"Rowan and I ... that is, magic in Fairhaven isn't fading," I say in a rush. "It's kind of the opposite, actually."

I explain that my parents used an ancient Egyptian healing spell to bind my sickness, but in doing so, they bound it to the magic of Fairhaven too, putting both behind a magical barrier. We've been able to use a small amount of magic, magic that's been seeping through or bubbling over somehow, but nothing big. None of my larger experiments ever worked. Nothing like the amount of magic it would take to heal Ruby.

"That's why we went to Boston, to Hawthorne College. We found a spell to undo the magic that my parents cast—"

"And it nearly killed you," Rowan interrupts, brow furrowed.

Stella and Jacque are more alert now, something like hope in their eyes, though they shudder at Rowan's words. I can't *bear* to see them suffer.

"Yes, but now we're *here*," I say. "I bet if we try it again …"

"No," Rowan says firmly. "Absolutely not."

"If we release the magic, then Stella can use it to heal Ruby," I argue.

"I've never attempted healing someone so sick," she says, frowning. "We'd need the coven. Temperance could help." She turns to Rowan. "She studied healing at Hawthorne before coming back and working as a nurse."

"You really think Hartwood would help you do a healing spell of this magnitude when a healing spell is what got you into trouble in the first place?" Jacque asks quietly.

Stella purses her lips. "She will," she says ominously.

"Maybe we could ask Thad for help too," I say.

Rowan shakes his head. "You're asking me to risk losing you, for the possibility of healing Ruby."

"I'm asking you to help me save my town, and my niece," I correct him.

Our eyes lock, both of us stubborn and unyielding.

"Let's at least meet with the coven," Stella says, her mind made up. "If there's any chance of unlocking the magic in Fairhaven and saving Ruby, I'll do it. Whatever it takes."

I squeeze her hand.

Whatever it takes.

CHAPTER 21

The coven meets at Stella's house later that evening. Everyone is somber, and the mood is hushed. Temperance, Agatha, and Madam Hartwood arrive together, a trio in formal black. Iris and Dahlia, Marigold, and the rest file in shortly after. The other children, Peony and River, have been left at home.

The house is dimmed, light coming only from the dozens of white candles that Stella and I have arranged around the first floor. The light flickers across the quartz crystal spires that Stella has collected over the years, casting the home in a warm glow, at odds with the icy feeling in my chest.

Madam Hartwood goes immediately to Stella upon entering the home, embracing her tightly. I'm fairly certain my jaw drops open in shock. She's wearing all black, like usual, but there's an almost maternal air to her tonight that I've never seen before on her stoic, wrinkled face. She cups Stella's face in her hands and whispers something to her that I can't hear. I exchange a surprised glance with Marigold, who shrugs, a weak smile trying to turn her lips.

The coven assembles in Stella's living room; Jacque has gone upstairs to be with Ruby, and the nurses have been sent home for the night. The living room is full of witches and familiars—cats, foxes, ravens, owls, one macaw, one golden retriever, and one stubborn little mouse—all of whom are quiet and solemn.

Rowan stands close beside me, his shoulder gently touching mine, and honestly, if looks could kill, I'd be dead a thousand times over from the daggers that Hartwood is glaring at me. I try to suppress a smug smile. Mean aunt or not, Rowan is in my life now. And I realize that I intend to do whatever I can to keep him in it.

"Thank you all for coming," Stella says. She swallows hard, the words sticking in her throat. "As you know, Ruby has been sick for … some time now. The doctors have done all they can, and they're saying that we need to prepare. That she's … she's probably going to die. And … soon."

A whisper of exclamations runs through the room, familiars shuffling and cawing and whining softly. Madam Hartwood's mouth purses, like she knows exactly what Stella intends to say next. Stella takes a deep breath, eyes catching on mine for a moment. I give her a nod of encouragement.

"I need your help," Stella says. "I tried to use magic in Philadelphia, but it wasn't strong enough. I need the magic of Fairhaven, of our coven, to help me heal my daughter. Please." Her voice cracks on the last word.

"This kind of healing magic is exactly what caused Fairhaven's magic to fail in the first place," Agatha Carrow reminds us, her voice like nails on a chalkboard.

Like we don't all already know that, I think.

A murmur of agreement runs through the room.

"Actually, the magic hasn't failed," Rowan says, pushing his glasses up on his nose, and I catch myself staring.

Since when have glasses been so attractive?

"It's only been bound," Rowan continues. "The aetherometer reading was off the charts. The ley lines are as potent as ever. They're just … blocked."

"Blocked? How? And by whom?" Hartwood asks.

A dozen heads swivel in my direction.

I explain. "The healing spell my parents used to save me, to bind illness from harming me … well, it bound the magic of Fairhaven too."

"So even if we wanted to use magic to help Ruby, we couldn't," Agatha says pointedly.

"Well, not yet. We could try lifting the spell—"

Rowan cuts me off, grabbing my hand.

"We tried lifting the spell already," he says, and there is a chorus of gasps from my coven. "It nearly killed Ivy. We need to find another way."

"Take her to Salem. You could try the healing spells there," Iris offers. Dahlia nods.

"She's too weak to move," Stella says, her voice no more than a whisper—but it silences the room.

I think of how frail Ruby is, how taxing it would be to take her to Salem now. Before, maybe, but now …

"Is it possible …?" Temperance says quietly, her voice like the rustling of dry leaves.

We all pause to look at her, with her tightly bound gray hair and gnarled hands. She's a formidable witch, even at her age, and the one of us with the most medical experience, magical and nonmagical.

"Is it possible that the bound magic itself is what's causing Ruby's symptoms?"

Stella's eyes go wide, and she looks at me with a terrified glance.

"I mean," Temperance says quickly, "the rainbow, the green fire. Magic has been trying to warn us."

"To warn us that Ivy is the problem!" Agatha cries. "The fire was as green as her hair!"

"And the ghosts have all gone," Iris says.

I freeze. I'd forgotten that Iris and Dahlia's family had ghosts as well.

"Granny's been missing too," I say.

Dahlia crosses her arms emphatically, giving a sideways glance to her mother.

Iris sighs.

"What's next? A plague of frogs?" someone exclaims.

An argument breaks out, witches yelling at each other, blaming me, blaming the bound magic, blaming each other.

Then Salem does the strangest thing. He jumps into the air, yowling like he's just been shot, and bolts from the room. Mabel starts whining, and Cinder scrabbles up my shirt and clings tightly to me. *What has gotten into them?* For a moment, the arguments subside as we all try to comfort our familiars. Flossy flies in a spiral around the room, narrowly missing us. My head aches, and a tremor runs through me—

No. The tremor shakes the entire room, jarring the walls, dust pluming into the air. Temperance shrieks, and the familiars join her. The cats race in circles, the foxes howl and moan. The crystal chandelier overhead clinks and rattles. On the bookshelf and fireplace mantel, the crystals overturn, one obelisk falling to the floor and shattering. Stella runs immediately to the staircase on wobbly legs, falling twice, and scrambles up the stairs on her hands and knees.

Rowan grabs me, and we hold each other as the floor rolls underneath our feet, like we're standing on the deck of a ship. Mabel leans against us; Cinder now clings to my hair. Agatha falls down, and Iris and Dahlia swoop in to help her. *We need to get out of the house!* I think. Or maybe I scream it—with all the noise, it's hard to tell.

But the earthquake is over in a minute, maybe two. It feels like a lifetime. The house creaks a little, but nothing falls, nothing more breaks or topples.

Rowan and I still cling to each other. For a moment, I'm lost in his eyes, blue and serious and sad all at once.

Then I see Hartwood glaring at me around his shoulder, and I let him go. I smooth back my hair self-consciously. The coven takes a few moments as we check to make sure everyone is all right. Iris and Dahlia have helped Agatha into a chair, where she sits angrily, chest heaving, and glares at me.

Everyone takes a few more moments to calm themselves and their familiar. Flossy is perched on the chandelier and does not move until Stella comes back down the stairs, and then she soars in a flutter of colorful feathers over to Stella's shoulder. Mabel is sitting at Rowan's feet, whining, despite Rowan trying his best to comfort her. The rest of the coven keeps shooting dirty glances in my direction, like this tremor was my fault too.

It does make me wonder, though.

What's next?

"Is Ruby all right?" Marigold asks.

Stella nods, wiping a weary hand across her face. "She's fine. Jacque's fine. She didn't even … didn't even wake." Her voice breaks.

I put an arm around her waist, and she leans against me, like all the strength has left her body. *Goddess, I need to convince the coven that we need to do this!*

"Ruby's claiming is in two weeks! This can't be a coincidence," Agatha continues in a harsh whisper, one bony finger pointed at me in blame.

There's a chorused murmur of agreement.

"Hey, I'm the one asking for your help lifting the spell!" I say.

Marigold clears her throat. "It's an Egyptian spell, you say?"

I nod.

She considers for a moment, stroking her giant cat, Biscuit, in her arms. Egyptians worshipped cats. I imagine Biscuit approves.

"So, if I understand you correctly," Marigold says, "if we lift Ivy's parents' spell, then magic will return to Fairhaven, and Ruby will be healed, or at least we can try to heal her ourselves."

We all murmur agreement.

"Okay. But also, if we lift the spell, then the protection Ivy has had all these years goes away, and she could die? Or her cancer could come back?"

Rowan stills beside me.

"It's … a possibility," I say, and a cold shiver runs through me. A risk I'm willing to take. My life for Ruby's and the magic of Fairhaven? Sounds like a fair trade to me.

"Could we, maybe …" Marigold stops, lowering her head, whispering something to Biscuit. She appears to agree with whatever Marigold asked, bumping her head against Marigold's chest.

"Well? Spit it out," Agatha commands.

"Well, if we lift the spell, Ivy … um, won't do well," Marigold says, face turning red. "So what if we don't lift it? But maybe … like, move it? Can we shift the spell's binding from all magic in Fairhaven to … what did the Egyptians use? Like an urn or something? Contain it, like a genie in a bottle?"

"Or in a crystal?" Stella says eagerly. "That would be stable enough." She grips my hand hard.

"Surely *someone* has used this spell before and not bound their entire city for all eternity," Temperance says acidly.

"So, not removing the spell," Rowan says, as if to himself. "Simply shifting its focus, changing its boundaries." He nods. "It might work."

"It has to," I tell him firmly. "Because one way or another, we're doing this."

"I appreciate your fervor, but let's be smart about this," Madam Hartwood says, her mouth pinched. "We have not attempted a spell of this magnitude since … since … well, *your* healing spell."

I shrug.

"We should research Egyptian spells, then," Temperance says, and I'm astonished that she's actually agreeing to this.

"We can talk to Thad at Hawthorne," I tell them. "He's a researcher there."

Temperance sniffs. "I'm something of an expert in Egyptian spell-work myself," she says. "And *I* studied healing at Hawthorne too."

"We could use all the help we can get," Marigold says gently.

Temperance's face softens a little.

"Madam Hartwood, do you still have the grimoires?" Dahlia asks.

Hartwood nods hesitantly.

"Mom and I can start going through them, with all your permissions," Dahlia says, nodding to the group. "There's at least one Egyptian witch in our ancestry. We may be able to find something there."

"I think," Iris says hesitantly, shooting a glance at Dahlia, "um, maybe instead, we should consider a séance. You know, to see if we can reach our ghosts. They may be able to tell us more about what's going on."

My breath catches in my chest. No one has done a séance in years—at least, not that anyone has admitted to. I can hardly believe it when Hartwood gives Iris a terse nod. Iris lets out a breath too, like she was afraid of Hartwood's reaction. This approval gives everyone hope, and some momentum, and soon we're all discussing ideas.

"I'm no good with séances," Dahlia says with a shrug, but she gives her mom a smile. "You can handle that. I'd be more use with the grimoires."

Iris gives her a fond hug around the shoulders, while Dahlia rolls her eyes at the motherly affection.

"I'll have the books brought here immediately," Hartwood proclaims, like even she is caught up in the excitement.

"I ... um, I still have mine," Marigold says sheepishly, turning red. "But I'll bring it over."

"And I have mine," Stella says firmly. Then she elbows me in the ribs.

I sigh. "I have mine too," I admit.

Hartwood rolls her eyes dramatically at us, like she's not the least bit surprised.

"I'll help Ivy with her grimoires, and we'll reach out to Hawthorne College as well," Rowan says, leaving no room for disagreement.

I'm glad. At least I get him for a little while longer.

"I'll contact the Concord," Agatha offers. "The High Priestess needs to hear about this. She and I go way back."

"It's settled, then," Madam Hartwood proclaims, stroking Salem in her arms, and the coven quiets. "Let us meet again tomorrow evening, to discuss our progress."

On the drive back to my apartment, I'm talking a mile a minute. I'm going to get out my old thread magic books. Knot magic was used even in ancient Egypt, and I'm betting I can find a way to use my magic to fix this. Though it's already late, I'm not tired at all.

Rowan is quiet as we drive, which I only realize when we pull up to my shop and I finally stop talking. I look up at the dark building before me, at my shop and my apartment. Cinder stirs in my pocket— she's been asleep for an hour—and I know Marvin is waiting for me upstairs.

But somehow, knowing Rowan will be gone soon, I already feel lonely. I release my seat belt but pause with my hand on the door.

"Um, thank you. For driving. And everything," I blurt out.

Rowan nods, one hand still on the gear shift.

"You're welcome," he says. "Ivy—we'll figure this out. I promise. I'll be by first thing in the morning, and we can get to work."

His words echo inside me, but instead of the sounds getting softer, the feelings get louder and louder.

"Wouldyouliketocomeup?" I blurt out.

He freezes.

"Um, if you want to, I mean. I know Hartwood's probably expecting you back at the mansion, but—"

I'm cut off by Rowan's lips crashing onto mine, by his strong arms dragging me from my seat until I'm practically straddling him in the car. I run my hands through his golden curls, which are just as soft as I imagined. I feel the strength of him, the hard muscles of his arms, the grip of his hands on my thighs. I need more. I need to feel something, *anything*, that isn't sadness and sickness.

Even if he'll be gone soon.

We break apart an eternity later, breathless, panting. His hands squeeze my legs, his head dropping to my shoulder with a groan.

"Is that a yes, then?" I ask.

"Yes," he murmurs against my skin, his lips grazing my neck, my collarbone. "Goddess, I need you. I need you in my arms. The thought of anything happening to you, of losing you ..."

I silence him with another kiss before opening the driver-side door and taking his hand.

We go up to my apartment together.

We're a mess of tangled limbs and moans and frantically ripped-off clothing by the time we finally stumble into my bedroom and collapse together onto the bed. Rowan traces every inch of my skin with his hands, like he's worshipping me, like he's memorizing me. But I'm not worried. One way or another, this will all be over soon—the curse my parents left on this town, the fear we've been living in, the pain poor

Ruby has been suffering through. My own health is only a small flicker of fear—medicine has come a long way since I was a child. Even if my leukemia comes back, I'll have that—plus the collective knowledge of Hawthorne College—on my side.

Rowan, however, is less certain, which does give me pause. If someone as brilliant and well read as my word warlock is uncertain about our success, well, I probably should be too.

But then I'm too caught up in his kisses, and in the way he looks at me when we're both spent, sweating and panting, our hands—and heart lines—entwined. He looks at me like I'm the most important thing in the entire universe, and—for a moment—I believe it.

CHAPTER 22

When I wake up in the morning, it's with sunshine pouring in through my window, Rowan curled around me, and Mabel's long tongue licking my face.

"Sorry about her," Rowan mumbles.

Mabel jumps onto the bed, tail wagging, trying to snuggle her big, fluffy body into bed with us. Cinder watches us from her bed on my nightstand with a look that I can only describe as exasperated and judgmental.

Rowan has a look around my bedroom for the first time, his sharp eyes taking in the elaborate quilt on the bed—mostly on the bed, anyway—the macrame art hanging on the walls, the needlepoint portrait of Cinder I made a few years ago. His gaze snags on a poofy bit of sequined black tulle poking out of the closet, and he gets up to investigate, wearing only a pair of gray boxers. He's lean, my word warlock, with a little softness around the middle from long days spent reading, and a spread of freckles across the fair skin of his shoulders and upper chest. As I'm admiring him, he grabs his glasses and heads over to look in the closet.

"What's this?" he asks, pulling the tulle skirt into the light of the bedroom.

I wrap the bedsheet around myself and go over to him, brushing hair back from my face.

"I like making clothes. Not just for my clients but for me too," I say, a faint blush heating my cheeks.

Will he find me weird now? I feel terribly self-conscious, though I try to fight it. *I'm a thread witch, for the goddess's sake. Of course I make clothes.*

He glances through the left side of the walk-in closet, which is

195

mostly old cosplay costumes. In the back, barely sparkling, is the dress I wore last winter solstice. If he notices the trace of magic on it, he doesn't comment—not that it matters now, I guess.

He instead picks out the purple dress I wore on Beltane.

"I like this one," he says, one finger tracing the low neckline, and it's his turn to blush.

I grin, feeling triumphant. It's nice to know it had the intended effect.

He puts it back, long fingers trailing over knitted sweaters and velvet dresses as he moves, like he's memorizing these pieces of me too. Next, he pulls out a little golden silk dress that barely deserves the name, as it more closely resembles a negligee, with thin straps and lacy accents. His eyes light up.

"This one next time, I think," he says.

I grin, reaching out to grab the offending item from him, and find myself once more tangled up in his kisses, before we tumble back into bed.

Eventually Rowan throws on his clothes and takes Mabel out for a quick walk. I stretch, grinning to myself at the mess my bedroom is in. Most of the sheets are on the floor, as are my clothes from last night. I can't bring myself to care.

By the time Rowan and Mabel are back, I've showered and dressed, and the mood is more somber. He picked up breakfast while he was out, so I enjoy Song's strong coffee, and croissants from Marigold's Bakery, with her famous honey butter.

We spend the morning on research—Rowan on his laptop, with a couple of phone calls to Thad, and me in my own magic books, now pulled out from their storage boxes. I have several compendiums of thread magic, so I start with those. I try not to think about the gold dress in my closet, and the way Rowan said *next time*. Would there be a next time? If we can't fix Fairhaven—or even if we do ...

"Hey, listen to this," I say, determination settling into me, and I bring one of the larger books into the kitchen.

Marvin follows me like a nervous puppy, sometimes patting my leg with a branch. I think he/she misses having Granny around. *She'll be back soon*, I think. As soon as we're done with all this. And then we can figure out what to call Marvin now that I know he's a girl.

"Look at this. It's from the Egyptian *Book of the Dead*," I say, placing it beside Rowan.

His hand drifts to my hip as I read.

Spell for a knot amulet of red jasper. "You have your blood, O Isis; you have your power, O Isis; you have your magic, O Isis." As for him for whom this is done, the power of Isis will be the protection of his body, and Horus, son of Isis, will rejoice over him when he sees him; no path will be hidden from him, and one side of him will be towards the sky and the other towards the earth. A true matter; you shall not let anyone see it in your hand, for there is nothing equal to it.[1]

"It's for something called a Knot of Isis, or *tyet*," I tell him.

He pulls the book over to look at the passage.

"Yes, yes, I think I've heard of it," he says, one finger tracing the words. "Usually it is carved, but I think, in your case, a literal knot in this configuration ..."

"Might take the boundary of my parents' magic and contain it in a knot instead?" I ask.

Rowan nods slowly, then stops. "You know this spell is meant to protect the body of the dead."

I nod and swallow.

"And you are, in fact, not dead," he continues.

I nod again. *Not dead, but only half-alive until we figure this out.*

"Do you think we can adapt it for the living?" I ask.

Rowan is silent.

"Let me talk to Thad," he says, reaching for his phone. He starts writing on a notepad: *Invoke gods of healing and balance—Isis, Thoth, Ma'at.*

I reach for mine as well and text Stella.

. . .

Do you have any red agate?

Red jasper, carnelian, I have them all. Why?

We might be onto something.

I bite my lip, then continue.

How's Ruby?

There's a pause. I know Stella has her phone in her hand—I can see those three little dots flashing as she types, then probably deletes her words and types again. That can't be a good sign.

The sooner we're done with this, the better.

Please tell me your plan keeps you safe too. I couldn't bear to lose you both.

I place my phone face down. If I keep looking at it, I know I'm going to start crying, and I can't afford to do that right now. I have things to do, damn it. A problem to solve, and then a warlock to seduce again, and again, and goddess knows how many purse orders and cosplay costumes I have in a backlog to do … These thoughts are the only things that keep me from completely breaking down. I'm worried sick for Ruby.

I try not to think about a scenario where I'm no longer a part of her life.

"Thad thinks it'll work," Rowan says triumphantly, and I take a deep breath, willing away my dark thoughts. "He's sending me everything he can on the *tyet*. He recommends Egyptian flax or cotton, if you have it."

I have a box of threads, cords, ropes, yarns, strings and more under my bed with my collection of witchy artifacts. I haven't gone through it in years, but I'm confident I have something that will work. I dig it out and start sorting the knotted mess left by my teenaged hands while Rowan and Thad work on the wording for our spell.

As the sun begins to set, Rowan and I set off for the town center, the mayor's garden, hand in hand. I have a length of Egyptian cotton cord in my pocket. I'm fairly certain it came from someone's curtains at some point, but it will do. We cleansed it with oil of frankincense and the burning of a black candle to symbolize the clearing of negative energies. It felt strange, doing magic again.

But it felt right too. I could feel the small curls of magic, like Cinder when she fidgets in my pocket for a comfortable spot. I can only imagine the strength we'll be able to feel when the barrier is down. The small spells I've attempted have largely been successful, but we'll need more than oils and candles to heal Ruby. Determination settles into me.

And there's something else. Something I haven't told Rowan.

I *am* prepared to die tonight.

The more I think about it, the more right it feels. I've been living these years on borrowed time. I never married, never left Fairhaven, never did anything, really, except my work. I've just been … half-alive. Like I always knew this day would come, and the scales would have to be balanced.

Cinder stirs in my pocket—my chest aches, knowing that when I die, she will too. It's not fair that someone so small and innocent has to pay the price of my curse. Tears well up in my eyes, and I cover the pocket with my hand, feeling her strong little warm body against my cold fingers. I swear she can read my mind, tell the direction of my thoughts. She scurries out and sits on my shoulder, giving my earlobe a little nibble and offering a soft squeak of encouragement.

I'm here, she's saying. *Let's do this.*

My little mouse is braver than I am.

We're met in the garden by the rest of the coven. The lamps have just flickered on, and the last of the day's casual guests are leaving— probably encouraged by Temperance's frowning face.

"Here," Marigold says, coming up and handing me a miniature cinnamon bun. "I baked these special, with a little extra magical courage." She's wearing black, like the rest of the coven, and her unruly blond curls are pulled back by a headband. She looks pale, but that could be the flour on her cheeks.

"Really?" I ask, and I pop it into my mouth. It's a bite of sugar and cinnamon and butter and, honestly, just bliss.

"Well, no," she says. "I don't know how to actually do that. It's just a cinnamon bun. But no one should have to go through something like this on an empty stomach!"

I can hear the fear in her voice. Her baking magic might not help much tonight, but having my friend Marigold by my side makes me feel instantly better. I give her a hug, and she squeezes me tightly.

Stella appears last, a silent waif. She hands me a black velvet draw-string bag—inside are the stones she promised, in obelisks and orbs and raw crystal formations.

I give her a wordless hug. She feels frail in my arms, like she's been losing weight.

"Ruby?" I ask.

Stella shakes her head, her lips pinched. "She's harder to wake up," she says, so quietly it's nearly a whisper.

I grip her hand tightly. "We're going to do this," I say, as confidently as I can.

She nods, too overcome with emotions to say anything else.

We assemble in the center of the garden. Someone has already lit the metal firepit, or maybe it set itself on fire—it glows in a familiar emerald. Everyone eyes it a little warily. Dahlia, the most levelheaded of the entire group, walks the perimeter of the garden, sprinkling dried herbs from a satchel as she goes. Her magic extends to concealment, to keep curious eyes away from the garden tonight. Anyone looking in this direction will simply see a garden, and then have a very compelling urge to look at something else.

"I pray that you two have a plan, as the rest of us are, sadly, without," Madam Hartwood says pointedly, looking down her nose at me. She's decided to go all-out witch tonight, wearing her pointed hat to match her pointed expression. Salem curls around her ankles, for once ignoring Cinder.

Rowan takes my hand, which renders Madam Hartwood practically apoplectic.

"We do," he says firmly, and my own courage is bolstered by his.

I squeeze his hand, memorizing the way it feels, warm and strong and fitting mine like it was meant for me.

We gather around the green flames, our familiars quietly keeping us company. Even Flossy is uncharacteristically silent, a gloomy gargoyle with bright feathers on Stella's dark shoulder.

I draw the red stones from the pouch Stella brought, and Rowan arranges them around the firepit, leaving a piece of raw agate with cream and gold striations for me to hold. He's been working on the wording for the spell all afternoon, confirming it with Thad. As word warlocks, this is their specialty.

"Ready?" Rowan asks.

I nod.

He raises his arms to the sky.

I call upon Sekhmet, who strikes and who heals.
   I call upon Thoth, keeper of the divine script.
   I call upon Ma'at, she who weighs the heart and sets the scales true.

He leaves out Osiris and Anubis, the guardians of the dead. I don't know how powerful the old gods still are, but if they were strong enough to cause this curse, then they must be strong enough to break it.

I begin the *tyet*, a simple knot that looks like an Egyptian ankh with the arms turned downward. It's meant to be tied in cloth, but in rope is simple enough. I focus on my movements, on the intention of the words Rowan speaks. *Please don't pass out again*, I think.

The rest of the coven surrounds us. I can feel their energy joining ours, their magic flowing, in a way that I haven't felt in years. To know they have my back, that they want to help—even if we don't always agree—sends a flood of resolve through me.

And I call upon Isis, whose magic heals.
You have your blood, O Isis;
You have your power, O Isis;
You have your magic, O Isis.

I prick my finger and allow a drop of blood to fall into the fire. A wind flares up, stirring the green flames into a raging bonfire, whatever fuel feeding them clearly supernatural. I take a step back as the heat blasts my face, one hand curling protectively around Cinder.

Rowan never falters.

What was bound, I unbind.
What was lost, I return.
Health to your daughter,
Magic to the land.

I take the cord from my pocket. The simple white cotton becomes hot, though it does not catch fire. I don't let go, gritting my teeth as my hands begin to blister against it. I wrap it firmly around the red agate. It's a simple knot, easy enough to tie even if I weren't a thread witch—but the blistering magic of Isis flowing through it burns as hot as the fire, and it's hard to focus.

Let illness be cast into thread.
   Let the living heart remain untouched.
   Let the river of magic return to its course.
   So I speak.
   So it becomes.

"So mote it be," my coven echoes.

I finish the knot, letting the sides drape down. A completed *tyet*. The blisters on my hands have popped and run, the skin beneath oozing and painful—but no worse than that.

"Did it work?" Agatha croaks behind me.

I don't feel any different—would I know, if the ley lines had returned to their course?

Above us, clouds black out the moon and stars, and a great wind howls through the garden, sending plants and dirt flying through the air. Skirts and shawls flap, and Stella and the others with bird familiars hold their animals tightly to prevent them from being ripped away.

The green flames turn into a swirling, towering inferno, a hundred feet tall—a tornado of fire and magic.

Pain lances through me, through my heart, through to my very marrow, and my back bends into a painful arch as the breath is stolen from my lungs.

And then—

It all goes dark.

EPILOGUE

ROWAN

"Rowan! I need you," Jacque calls from somewhere in the massive kitchen.

Over the cluster of witches and familiars, I can barely see him. There's the entire home for people to spread out, but with Jacque's cooking—and Marigold's treats—everyone has crammed into the kitchen. I feel more at home with them all here than I ever did at Hawthorne College—it's like suddenly having a dozen aunts and sisters and cousins. As a child with emotionally distant parents and a singular asshole for a brother, the contrast is stark. And I've realized that I like it. I belong here. I've even invited Thad and Marta to visit.

As I move to help Jacque, everyone has a kind word or hug for me, now that I've decided to stay in Fairhaven. There are even some new faces here as witch families are returning, as the news of Fairhaven's healing has spread.

I grab the stack of plates and cloth napkins Jacque hands me and head outside. Stella's rented out tables and chairs and decorations so that the ceremony will be as beautiful as Ruby is. There are red roses everywhere—in vases, climbing on trellises, blooming and filling the air with soft fragrance.

Stella is back here too, nudging some of the flowers into ever-more-perfect arrangements. Flossy soars through the air, cackling in excitement.

"Flowers! More flowers!" Flossy calls.

Stella looks as polished as ever this evening, in sleek white pants and a red sweater—though there's a tightness around her eyes I don't remember seeing when we met. When she sees me, she takes the plates from my hands and starts setting them out automatically, like she's not really seeing them.

"It looks beautiful," I tell her. She stops in the middle of putting down a plate and turns to me.

"Does it?" she asks, sounding a little lost.

"It does," I confirm. "No one has ever had a more beautiful claiming party."

"Well, we're just glad you're here. After everything that has happened."

I flash back to the other night.

I've never been inside a tornado before, never mind one streaked with emerald fire, and I hope to the goddess I never will again. The blackness is near total, my only source of illumination the fire that whirls around us—around me and Ivy. The look of concentration on her face as her fingers blister and burn is something that I will never forget, not for as long as I live. Nor her stubborn insistence to set things right.

After she completes the knot, after the coven roars the conclusion of the prayer, so loudly I can hear it over even the winds—well, Ivy just ... falls. Like before, in the temple at Hawthorne College, when we tried to remove the spell.

Only this time, there is no shaking, no seizing.

She is just ... still.

The wind and fire have vanished, but I didn't really notice when. I leap for Ivy, my knees slamming against the paving stones as I reach for her. I lift her head from the ground, put my ear to her lips to see if she is breathing, watch her chest, wait for any inhalation, any indication that she is alive, that she is all right ...

The knot falls from her hands, stained and bloody. I smooth the hair back from her face. Aunt Patience and the others surround us, and Dahlia holds up her cell phone to give us light.

"Let me see her," Temperance says, kneeling at her side. She reaches for Ivy's wrist and feels a moment for a pulse. Her lips purse. My heartbeat stutters.

"You can't do this," I tell Ivy, my hands shaking where they cradle her head. My vision blurs, and I blink a few times to try to clear them. "You *can't*. Too many people here need you. *I* need you."

I love you.

Cinder clings to Ivy's shirt, over her heart, squeaking her own furious commands to her witch, her fur standing on end and one ear charred. Her tail whips back and forth, getting in Temperance's way, but she will not be moved.

Stella kneels by my side, quiet. Temperance holds a hand in front of Ivy's mouth, checking for breath.

Temperance shakes her head. She sighs, pushing back onto her knees, hands on her hips. Her mouth quivers, and she claps a hand over it before she can sob.

Beside me, Stella buries her head in my shoulder, her body shaking.

I smooth the hair back from Ivy's face again, dimly noticing the ribbon she tied in it today is gone. Of all things, that darned ribbon is what stands out to me at this time, and how hard it is going to be to find it after that storm.

After a moment, Aunt Patience comes to stand beside us, quiet. Then she lets out a breath, like she's decided something and it isn't pleasant. She pushes back her sleeves, her face set and determined.

"Well, there's only one thing left to do," she says.

Stella must be thinking about that night too. She throws her arms around me in a move that has me more than a little off-balance. Mabel thinks this is an invitation to play and bounces around us with a happy bark.

"If you break her heart, I will kill you myself," Stella whispers into my ear.

I swallow. No need to ask what she's talking about.

"Noted," I say, pushing my glasses back into place.

She releases me, gives me a practiced and perfectly whitened smile, and goes back to rearranging flowers.

I rub a hand across the back of my neck. I don't doubt the witch's intentions for a second. Her loyalty to Ivy is intense. Ever since I've practically moved in with Ivy—adding a magical extension to her apartment for my library, of course—well, I understand it entirely. And Granny was only too pleased to welcome me after she'd been released from the ley lines, especially when I cooked Italian.

On impulse, I grab a rose from the nearest vase and whisper some words over it. The petals change from velvety red to soft blue and lavender with a crown of yellow in the middle.

"Kind of clashes with the red, don't you think?"

Ivy appears at my side, her green hair curled and crowned with small white flowers, no evidence of the other night's magic visible at all. The only remnant is an agate wrapped in Egyptian cotton cord in a locked box in Ivy's closet. Ivy has remained blessedly healthy, and she swats at me every few hours when she catches me watching her too closely for any signs of ill effects.

I will never be able to repay Aunt Patience for healing my Ivy. For her and the coven, coming together, their magic twining with the newly released superpotent magic of the ley lines to bring her back to us, to bring her back to me.

If they had thought for even a moment that using this much magic, this soon, was going to harm the ley lines again, was going to sap them the way they'd thought they'd been drained before—well, no one hesitated for even a heartbeat.

Tonight Ivy is wearing a silver dress that turns deep green every few minutes, and then back again, and shoes that look like glass. Her magic is present in every stitch, every thread, and it shows. Tonight she's showing off exactly how beautiful and wondrous magic can be, just like it used to be.

But even when she's naked—no, *especially* then—she's easily the most beautiful creature I've ever seen.

"I promised you flowers the next time I took you on a date," I say, handing her the lotus.

She smells it, her cheeks flushing pink.

"You did," she says, looping her arm through mine.

I stoop and drop a kiss on her lips, only interrupted by Jacque calling out from the kitchen door—"*It's time!*"

There's a rush of witches onto the back patio. Some of them, like Aunt Patience, wear traditional black. Others, though, like Marigold and Dahlia, wear clothing that Ivy has made for them. Flowers bloom and swirl across Marigold's skirts like they're blowing in a breeze, and Dahlia's black corset glitters like it's made of scales. Even Temperance is wearing a bright silk ribbon around her hat brim tonight, which ties itself into elaborate bows every few minutes. There's more color on her cheeks than I've ever seen, likely the effect of the wineglass that Jacque surreptitiously refills when she isn't looking.

Ivy and I take our seats near Stella. Mabel curls up at our feet, exhausted from playing fetch with River, and Cinder rustles happily in a nest she's made of our napkins. Aunt Patience approaches and, when she reaches us, pauses and clears her throat.

"There's … something I wanted to say. To you," she says, addressing Ivy.

Ivy stills beside me. She's always nervous around my aunt and hasn't forgiven her for the years of mistrust between them.

"I … that night. The night your parents died. You lost your parents that night, but I … also lost my friends," she says, her thin voice catching for a moment.

Salem curls around her ankles encouragingly.

"I … I just wanted to say. I regret that this … pain drove us apart, when it could have brought us together."

Ivy's mouth drops open in surprise. Mabel lets out a little woof of surprise herself, startling Salem into a hiss.

Ivy extends her hand, and Aunt Patience grabs it quickly, like she's afraid Ivy is going to change her mind.

"Tonight is a good night for a new beginning," Ivy says.

My aunt's eyes fill with tears, and she looks away, sniffling. She pretends to be checking the status of the full moon, just now peeking over the trees, but I know her better than that. It warms my chest to see her trying to mend her relationship with Ivy. After all, we're going to be one family soon, if I have anything to say about it.

"Yes. Well. Enjoy the party," Aunt Patience says, and she walks off.

Ivy looks up at me, hazel eyes wide, but before we can even try to understand what just happened, a hush falls over the coven.

Ruby enters the backyard like a princess. Ivy has made her a gown of red tulle and sequins, and a tiara to match. Actually, I doubt any princess in history ever looked as radiant as Ruby does tonight, glowing with her family's love—and in perfect health.

She walks to the center of the yard, where a circle is marked out in salt and rosemary. A small table is set with a dish of milk and honey, to welcome her familiar, and with unlit candles—red, blue, green, and yellow, but also black, white, and purple. Ruby walks to the circle and turns to face us, her hands clasped in front of her, a wide and slightly anxious smile on her face.

Tonight is the night her power will reveal itself—as well as her familiar.

Aunt Patience stands and begins the incantation. The rest of the coven joins, speaking the familiar words in strong voices.

By moon and moss, by claw and wing,
We call the one who is listening.
Through gentle heart and steady hand,
Come walk beside her on this land.

A soft wind stirs the roses and rustles the plush green grass of the yard. Ivy grips my hand tightly, her eyes fixed on her niece, her body practically vibrating with energy beside me.

A twinkling of light, then another, and another, as dozens of flecks of silver light swirl around Ruby—it's magic, recognizing her and welcoming her. They reflect off the sequins of her dress and off the gems in her tiara, surrounding her with light. It's a beautiful scene—I've been to a few claimings beside my own, but this one feels different. Special. Like all of us here, the Fairhaven coven, united—like the magic is somehow sentient, and pleased to be free of its bonds again.

The lights pulse, brighter, and then finally coalesce …

When the light clears, Ruby's familiar is revealed.

There's a tiny dark creature crouching at her feet.

"Oh," Ruby coos, scooping to pick it up. "I'm going to call you … Midnight."

The kitten, a fluffy black one with pumpkin-orange eyes and a sweet flattened face, meows loudly in agreement, and the coven bursts into cheers. Stella and Aunt Patience exchange a glance, as if relieved that Ruby's familiar is a cat and not something more … exotic. Ivy and I secretly placed bets. Ivy was hoping for a red panda. I was thinking maybe a peacock.

Another gathering of sparkles, another collective holding of the coven's breath—and this time the sparks settle on the unlit white candle. The candle flickers into life in response and then burns in steady flame.

"Healing!" Stella crows triumphantly, excited and relieved and also now crying. She falls dramatically into Jacque's arms, while he smiles and laughs and shouts encouragements to Ruby.

Ruby beams, cuddling Midnight and whispering to him, no doubt all her plans for their future together. The kitten appears absolutely smitten with her and keeps bumping his little head against her chin.

Ivy leans into my side, and I wrap my arm around her. The little purr of contentment she makes as she snuggles in close is a sound I know I'll never get enough of. I drop a kiss on her green hair, and silently thank the goddess—and Dahlia's palmistry app—for bringing us together.

THE END

BIBLIOGRAPHY

1. Faulkner, Raymond O., Ogden Goelet, Carol Andrews, J. Daniel Gunther, and James Wasserman. *The Egyptian Book of the Dead: The Book of Going Forth by Day: The Complete Papyrus of Ani Featuring Integrated Text and Full-Color Images*. 20th anniversary revised and expanded edition. San Francisco: Chronicle Books, 2015.
2. Ball, Pamela. *The Book of Practical Witchcraft: A Compendium of Spells, Rituals, and Occult Knowledge*. Sirius Publishing, 2023.

ACKNOWLEDGMENTS

I couldn't possibly have accomplished this book without my "real-life book boyfriend," my husband. From being the first person to read each draft, to building me more bookshelves to house my horde of books — thank you. Thank you for always having my back, for being my biggest supporter and #1 fan.

For my beta and ARC readers, and the readers who continue to read and love my books — your support means the world to me. I never could have imagined that so many people would read my stories in my wildest dreams.

For my editor, Leonora Stewart; my cover artist, Honei Studio; thank you for the care and love you have shown for this book. I can't wait to see what we come up with for the next one!